Black Hand Over Kansas

Black Hand Over Kansas

by

Ernest C. Frazier

ERNEST C. FRAZIER

1802 Hoover Way, Dodge City, Ks. 67801-2616
E-Mail: speed@pld.com

ISBN 1-58500-280-1

This book is printed on acid free paper.

1stBooks-rev. 4/20/01

CHAPTER 1

CHINA 1865

A tiny farm stood alone on the northern border of China. There, in the pre-dawn gloom, a peasant and his wife milked their goats. The rising sun drove away a heavy fog and replaced it with an eerie glow. Always alert to the possibility of danger from the north, and now able to see for a short distance, the nervous couple glanced toward the mountains. They stopped milking and stood up for a better look. Less than a quarter of a mile away, a vision shimmered in the haze. Fascinated, they stared in awe. In a moment, however, the fog evaporated and their fascination gave way to horror. They knew that death was coming today. A thousand Mongol horsemen, the troops of the warlord, Sol Ping, were standing motionless in the mist. The paralyzed couple watched as Sol Ping's stallion reared up on its' hind legs. A silver sword thrust high in the air. A ram's horn sounded. The peasant's wife collapsed and pitched forward on the ground. Unleashed, the screaming hordes poured across the border. Their initial target was an outpost less than twenty miles away, manned by the guards of Ke Li, their sworn enemy. They planned to overrun the outpost, then sweep inland to his fortress and put Ke Li to the sword, thus securing his province for themselves. Able-bodied captives would be enslaved. The others would be massacred. The peasant fell across the body of his wife and waited.

A day later and a hundred miles to the south, Ben Wang buried his head in his pillow. Not yet awake, he ignored the pealing of a massive gong, relegating the noise to the deepest recesses of his mind. The racket intensified, demanded attention, and finally pierced his veil of slumber. He bolted upright, wide eyed as he grasped the situation. *The alarm! The alarm!* He jumped out of bed, jerked the cover off his bride and screamed, "Su Chang! Wake up! We are under attack!"

"What?" his groggy wife mumbled as she rolled out of bed. "What is happening?"

"Get dressed! Now! The alarm gong is sounding!"

Outside, throngs of panicked people were pouring into the compound of their protector, the warlord, Ke Li. On top a twenty-foot watchtower, a sentry rhythmically banged his mallet against a massive gong. Three hundred yards away, the doors to Ke Li's private stables swung open. The warlord, escorted by a dozen guardsmen, spurred their horses to the tower.

Ke Li leaped from the saddle, silenced the gong with a wave of his hand, and climbed to the top of the tower.

His voice boomed out to the hushed crowd. "My informants have brought terrible news! The forces of Sol Ping have overrun our northern border. Our guard has been slaughtered to the last man! The Mongols will be upon us before another day passes!"

Ben felt as though he'd taken a blow to the stomach. He glanced at his mother, Mi Chan. The news had drained her face of blood. Her husband, Ben's father, was a captain in the border guard! Ben reached out to steady the shaken woman, but she pulled away and stared blankly ahead.

Their grief would have to wait. Ke Li continued, "We have no time to lose. You know our escape route. We flee immediately. Anyone left here will die! Disperse and prepare to leave! We have not one minute to spare!"

Ben was stunned. His uncle, Ke Li, had fought for and conquered this province years ago. Ben's family had been awarded exclusive rights to distribute all silk in the province. It turned out to be a bonanza as Ben's shrewd business skills made his family very wealthy. Now, they had no choice but to grab what they could and run away from it all. He stepped between his wife and mother, took their arms, and rushed them back to their quarters. The stunned women said nothing. He thought of his father and the men under his command. He knew they had been decimated by smallpox and had no replacements to fill their ranks. *Little wonder they fell under the onslaught of the Mongols. My mother will never rest until my father's bones are retrieved.*

His mind quickly returned to the problem at hand. Their escape. Fortunately they had a well-rehearsed plan and everyone swung into action. The compound looked like a beehive under attack. Within minutes, dozens of horses and camels were saddled. Others were harnessed to small carts to haul women, children, and household goods. Freight wagons would follow loaded with dried pumpkins, rice, grain and water for man and beast alike.

The pace was feverish. The terrified villagers were all too familiar with the ways of the Mongols. They would come swiftly, sweeping across the plains, torching every village in their path. The fleeing populace would be ridden down without mercy, their bodies impaled on lances along the road to stand in mute testimony to the power of Sol Ping.

Within minutes, Ben's family had loaded a cart with silks, precious stones, artifacts, and household belongings. Then Ben lit and tossed a torch into their sleeping quarters. The Mongols would find nothing but the ashes of the compound when they arrived.

A guardsman banged the gong again and bellowed out, "Stop packing! Set your fires and get in line! We march!"

A hundred or more torches were thrown into the half empty quarters and everyone scrambled to their carts. Ben's wagon was positioned near the middle of the column.

As they pulled out, everyone looked back, shielding their faces against the rising flames. Their village would be nothing but a memory in a matter of minutes.

"Are we really going all the way to America?" Su Chang choked out as their cart lurched forward. She knew that was the plan but it was hard to believe.

Ben nodded his head; "Ke Li knows that great fortunes can be made in California by our people, especially tradesmen who bring money. Yes, we will go there. The time is right. There are no lands for us here. Ke Li's plan is for us to escape to the province of Song Chen. In exchange for a chest full of silver, Song Chen's armies will hold off the Mongols and provide soldiers to escort us to Shanghai. From there, we'll sail to San Francisco."

He cracked his whip in the air. The caravan was already picking up speed. Women, riding in pony carts with their children, began sewing money into their bulky clothing and heavy quilts. The men carried only small sums on their persons so they could pacify any roadside bandits. While they were escorted by Ke Li's guards, they couldn't afford the time for unnecessary confrontations. Payoffs would be cheap compared to a loss of time and manpower. Ivory, jade and other precious stones were concealed in barrels of grain and of rice. They rode night and day without rest, only stopping to replace their worn out animals with fresh teams that trailed behind. After six days, they came within sight of the hills that marked the entry to Song Chen's province. The column was stringing out. The people had driven themselves and their animals beyond endurance. Their spirits rose when they saw the army of Song Chen waiting for them, massing on a hillside some three miles away.

But, their joy was short lived. A lone guardsman providing reconnaissance to their rear galloped in bellowing at the top of his lungs. "Faster! Faster! The Mongols are upon us!"

Everyone looked back. A huge column of dust was spiraling skyward not two miles behind. The Mongols were mounting a cavalry charge! Ke Li ordered his out manned guard to the rear. While women and children shrieked with terror, the men flogged their faltering animals in a last ditch effort to reach the protection of Song Chen's forces. Carts and wagons began falling apart, their wooden wheels breaking under the incessant pounding against the rock hard trail. Ben lashed his animals with a vengeance as they raced through the melee. Su Chang and her mother were screaming as cart after cart loaded with their friends crashed along the road. Ke Li, seeing the desperate plight of the victims, barked an order to the captain of the guard.

The guardsmen wheeled and charged straight into the Mongol hordes. Their strategy saved the main party. But, the price they paid was the ultimate. The guardsmen were overwhelmed by the Mongols in a matter of minutes.

The Mongols suddenly abandoned their attack as the troops of Song Chen rode into view. Having overrun the territory they coveted and now totally out manned, the Mongols fled back to the north.

The caravan, now led by Ke Li and three companies of Song Chen's troops, continued on to the seaport at Shanghai. They arrived in two weeks and booked passage on a clipper ship.

Sailing time to San Francisco would be six weeks, giving Ben and Su Chang time to plan to establish their silk business in California. Ben didn't know that from the moment he boarded the ship he was a marked man, the target of an extortion scheme. Their shattered lives were about to take another whirlwind turn. It would alter their lives beyond anything they'd ever dreamed of.

Five youths on the ship were pointed out as members of a Chinese secret society, The Tong of The Black Hand. Ben knew little of the organization. He thought it was little more than a merchant's social club cloaked in an aura of mystery. He was partially right. The tongs had organized in China as benevolent, but secret, societies operating for the betterment of their members. Over the years, however, the Tong of The Black Hand had been taken over by criminals and was now controlled by a powerful syndicate in China whose long tentacles reached San Francisco's teeming Chinatown. There, along with several lesser tongs, it controlled dozens of opium dens and all prostitution and gambling activities in the city. While they professed to be protectors of Chinese businessmen, they in fact extorted protection money from them to finance their illicit ventures. Failure to comply with their demands for cash resulted in either a beating, the burning of one's store, death, or the kidnapping of family members for ransom. The predominantly Anglo-Saxon police force of San Francisco saw no need to interfere with "Chinese business" and remained noticeably absent from the area. Also, a code of silence prevailed within the community. No one who valued his life informed on the tongs.

Ben, unfortunately, was ignorant of such facts. When he received a note requesting his presence at a tong meeting, he went to meet his mysterious hosts.

Five tongsmen ushered him into their cabin and nodded curtly for him to take a seat. Without any of the small talk that customarily preceded business discussions, the spokesman opened up by stating that they knew Ben was a wealthy silk merchant with plans to settle in San Francisco. The spokesman declared that they would provide protection for Ben. In exchange, Ben would pay them, in cash, fifty U. S. dollars twice each month.

"To show your good faith in our partnership," he explained, "we require your first payment now!"

Ben, astounded, rose from his seat.

"I pay no tribute! I escaped the Mongols to gain my freedom. I owe you nothing!" He moved toward the door. "Let me out of this cabin, now!" he demanded. He reached for the door but his adversaries were quick. A swinging back fist crashed into his face. Flashes of light exploded in his head as the cartilage in his nose gave way. He staggered back then dropped to one knee. Through his clouded vision he saw the tongsmen reaching for knives and clubs. Half conscious, he jerked his pistol from his smock. He lurched sideways as a club, swung with deadly force, bounced off his collarbone. His left arm went numb. Sensing he was a half second from death, he shoved his pistol into the belly of his assailant and pulled the trigger. The wounded man screamed in agony and fell back into the arms of his comrades.

The others dropped their weapons and backed away. Their clubs and knives were no match against gunfire. One of them dropped down and tried to staunch the flow of blood pouring from the man writhing on the floor. It did no good. The wounded man quit moving. His eyes rolled back in his head, then stopped, fixed in the stare of the dead. The others stood rigidly, staring at Ben as though memorizing his face. Ben, shocked by what he'd done, backed toward the door, his pistol shaking in his hand. The spokesman, his eyes as cold as steel, moved away from the door. "Only a fool challenges the authority of the Black Hand!" he said. "You have killed Han Fen, nephew of Kai Mang! From this day forward The Tong of The Black Hand will seek revenge! You and your family will never rest in peace! You will all die!" Having uttered those cryptic phrases, he stepped away from the waving pistol and allowed Ben to walk out.

Ben lurched back to his cabin on legs that felt like they were made of stone. Inside, he bolted the door and blurted out the whole story to his wife. She found difficulty understanding him. The flight from the Mongols had drained her mentally as well as physically. They agreed to wait until morning to tell Ben's mother about the danger they were in. She would be safe and well rested as her cabin door was always locked.

Throughout the night, Ben could hear Su Chang sobbing with fear. He could do little to comfort her.

Shortly after 6:00AM, just as they were getting up, they heard the ship's horns wailing a warning. It was followed by a cry from the watch, "Man overboard!"

The body of Mi Chan was recovered fifteen minutes later.

As Ben stood mute with shock, the ship's doctor examined his mother's body. He declared she had a broken neck and questioned Ben about the presence of deep bruises on her neck. The doctor surmised, that, if she fell overboard while taking a night turn around the deck, her neck may have broken either by hitting the side of the ship or by hitting the water at an awkward angle. He said it was not uncommon for unhappy travelers to leap into the sea, but he wondered about the bruises. Ben offered no answers except to sign a statement that Mi Chan who was recently widowed and in a depressed state of mind, may have taken her own life. The doctor accepted the explanation, entered the death as a suicide in his log, and released Ben from further questioning.

Outside, lounging by the ship's rail, one of the tong members was picking his fingernails with a dagger and enjoying the sunrise as it flooded the horizon. His unblinking eyes met Ben's as they passed on deck. Ben shuddered, thought about pulling his pistol again, then, thinking better of it, tabled the idea. He unlocked their cabin and was greeted by a silent message. The inked imprint of a small black hand was emblazoned on the door. Ben studied it for a moment. Something was odd about the hand. Then, it dawned on him. *The hand has six fingers!* He hurried in to check on Su Chang. She was there, unharmed. He told her of his mother's murder and the sign on the door. They decided they should consult with Ke Li at once.

Ke Li was well aware of the power of the tongs. He had maintained an uneasy truce with them in the past, but now, a refugee himself, he could exercise no bargaining power on behalf of Ben. The tongs simply wouldn't listen to him. However, he could offer some valuable advice. Also, the crafty warlord had a plan for their escape.

"You insulted the society by refusing to pay tribute and you killed the nephew of the powerful Kai Mang. Those are unforgivable actions. You are a rebellious person willing to stand against them, something most of our people would never do. To begin your punishment, they killed your mother. Then they left the sign on your door. A six fingered black hand marks one person for death--you. Su Chang, however, will be allowed to live. She killed no one, but, as your wife, she must suffer. If Kai Mang decrees it, she will be admitted to his harem. If not, she will be sold to a merchant dealing in female flesh-a white slaver who provides women for dens of pleasure on the Barbary Coast."

Ben interrupted and asked him to explain. Ke Li responded, "A slaver could pay the tong $15,000 for her and recover his investment in less than six months. From that point forward, all income earned off her is pure profit."

Ben, more distressed than Su Chang had ever seen, blurted out, "What can we do? How can we escape? We are trapped on this ship. In two days it will be docked outside San Francisco. We will have to spend ten days under quarantine before we can get off. Surely they will find a way to kill us before we ever get to dry land."

Ke Li answered, "I have a plan. Listen carefully. I have already spoken to Captain Van Dyke. He had strong suspicions that Mi Chan's death was not a suicide and was not surprised when I told him it was the work of the Black Hand. He is deathly afraid of the tongs and will go to any lengths to avoid trouble with them. He wants to get you off the ship tonight. An officer and two oarsmen will help you pack your belongings in a lifeboat. As soon as it is dark you will be taken aboard. The tongsmen will be kept busy by the doctor. He will examine them in his cabin as part of the quarantine procedure. They will not know of your departure. In the morning they will see a quarantine sign on your cabin stating that no one can enter due to smallpox. That will explain your absence from the ship's deck for several days."

"How is it possible that we can enter the harbor in an unauthorized vessel?" asked Ben, worried that they would be stopped and detained in San Francisco.

"Captain Van Dyke and his crew know the Harbor Master. They will allow the lifeboat safe passage. It will not be advisable for you to enter San Francisco at all since the tong has a mighty presence there. You will be docked many miles to the south at a small settlement which seldom sees a Chinese face. You can buy a horse and buggy from a trader there. The arms of the tong reach far so you must leave California and find a place to live in the interior. Avoid settlements populated by our people. Do not engage in the silk trade as you could be easily traced. Perhaps you could operate a restaurant." He nodded at Su Chang. "You used to work with your father in my kitchens." He turned back to Ben. "I will pay you a fair price for your silk as I can dispose of it in San Francisco. If you wish, I can store your precious stones until you call for them. It will not be safe to travel with them. Whenever you wish you may pick them up, or, notify me and I will sell them for you. I have a bank account in San Francisco which I can draw on to pay you for the silk. You can deposit that draft in any bank in the country."

Ben set a price, accepted a draft, and thanked Ke Li for the advice. That night, he, Su Chang, and the three crewmen, slipped over the side of the ship into the lifeboat. Two days later, they pulled into a tiny inlet, left the boat with the sailors and stepped onto California soil for the first time. An honest trader sold them three horses and a sturdy wagon with a canvas top. He told them of a wagon trail that would lead them eastward into the territories of Nevada and Utah, then on to Colorado. From there they could elect to go north to Wyoming, south to New Mexico, or east to Kansas. While settlements were springing up in all the territories, he told them that most of them were mining or cattle towns and were populated with gunslingers and outlaws. In his opinion, Kansas, while it had it's share of renegades, carpetbaggers, and other border ruffians, would provide more opportunity for a permanent location. Settlers there were establishing farms, ranches, and small towns. More important, almost no Chinese lived there.

So, the decision was made to head east across the Sierra Nevada Mountains into Nevada, make a beeline through Utah and Colorado Territories, then on into Kansas, a trip of six months.

The Shoshone Mountains of Nevada and the Wasatchs' of Utah provided the biggest challenges to their sturdy wagon. By staying on the well marked wagon trails and rotating pulling duties among their horses, they were able to enter southern Colorado on schedule, only to run straight into roaming bands of Ute Indians. Fortunately, the Indians were friendly and owned a good supply of horses. Ben traded his tiring animals for three young mares, freshly shod and ready for the trail.

They pulled off the trail in Durango and rented a room. They met a weather-beaten prospector who went by the nickname of Smooth Mouth Sam, or, just Smooth Mouth, as he'd lost his teeth as a boy. He told them he and his sons operated a mine in Arizona. He'd come to Durango to see a doctor, who, it was alleged, could cure his rheumatism. After four weeks of treatments, he felt a little better and was going back to Arizona. Ben and Su Chang, getting more proficient with their English every day, were happy to be able to talk with him. Upon hearing they were going to scout around Kansas for a place to settle, he suggested the town of Alexander.

He said, "I know an old boy down there named J. T. Smith. He went to Alexander from St. Joe. Used to outfit me when I'd come through. Sold me mules, dynamite, and everything else. If I was busted he'd put it on the cuff. Fact is, I was so broke last trip that I gave him a bunch of shares in my mine. He'll hold them shares until I can buy 'em back. They're legal stocks made out in my name 'cause I had a lawyer draw up the papers. I ain't never struck nothin' big yet, but, my boys are down there diggin' right now. I give J. T. a map of where we're workin' at and told him that, if I die out there mining, he should come and take a look. If we hit a rich vein, the mine will be worth a lot of money. If not, I guess he can collect from me in heaven, or maybe, hell, just depending where I land!" He chuckled at his own joke, spit a little tobacco on the floor and continued, "Anyway, he's a good old boy and he makes money wherever he goes. If Alexander, Kansas is good enough for J. T. Smith, it ought to be good enough for you. You'll make money there if you use your head. 'Course you'll probably have to shave off that top-knot off if you want anyone to trade with you." he guffawed at his little insult, a direct jab at the braid of hair extending from the crown of Ben's head down to the middle of his back. "They ain't no cowboy goin' to do business with a Chinaman with a haircut like that!"

That night Su Chang cut the queue off, giving Ben a more acceptable, if still an Oriental, appearance. Also, they decided to take the old prospector's advice and make a visit to Alexander.

When they pulled east out of Durango the next morning they

saw a wagon in the distance. It pulled by two mules and was taking the south fork out of town. "Is that Smooth Mouth Sam?" Su Chang asked. Ben strained his eyes to look. Then he caught a glimpse of something else and his heart started pounding. "I can't tell from here. Maybe it is, but look. Two horses are following him. Are those riders Chinese? They look like it."

Su Chang shielded her eyes from the rising sun and took a long look at the riders. "I don't think so, but even if they are, we have nothing to fear. They are going south and we are going east. No, I don't think they are Chinese."

Ben nodded his head and decided he was probably worrying unnecessarily. Without giving it another thought, they continued on toward the Continental Divide, the last gigantic barrier between them and the plains of Kansas. Wolf Creek Pass provided the only major trail. They crawled at a snail's pace up to the summit, a two-day trip in its own right. It was fall and the scenery was spectacular. The sun danced on the red, gold, and green leaves, playing tricks on their imaginations, conjuring up images of fire bursting out spontaneously on the mountains. They had never seen such sights on the flat, sterile plains of China, and vowed to visit the mountains again if the opportunity presented itself. They never suspected how soon that was going to happen. But, for now, there was little time to enjoy the view. The chill brought by the whisper of frost in the air warned them to waste no time. Snow would soon blanket the Rockies.

Thirty-five days later they rode into Alexander. Blank faces stared in wonder when they stopped at the livery stable. Less than ten percent of the settlers had ever seen a person from the Orient and their presence caused quite a stir.

After stabling their animals they obtained lodging at the Goodnite Inn. They found the Goodnites to be cordial hosts who were quite interested when Ben told them that it was their plan to open a restaurant in town.

"Look", Jack Goodnite said, "we've got a first class restaurant all ready set up. We just can't find anyone to operate it. Do you really know how to run a large restaurant?"

Ben explained that Su Chang's father had operated the kitchens for the warlord, Ke Li, and she had worked there. Ben could run a business and she knew how to run the kitchen.

That night, they agreed to lease the restaurant with an option to buy. They would live in a suite on the second floor of the hotel. The next morning, Goodnite took Ben around town and introduced him to some of the more prominent citizens. In particular Ben wanted to meet the banker, Chester Zimmerman, not to borrow money but to open an account.

When they'd completed their tour of Main Street, Ben met Chester. After some small talk Goodnite left them alone to talk business.

Chester said he'd welcome their business. After several questions, Ben discovered the bank was not chartered since it was short one stockholder/investor, but had authority to operate for twelve months until one could be found. This satisfied Ben, especially when Chester signed an agreement stating that their money would be returned if the charter were not obtained. Having the assurance that his money would be safe, Ben opened his account with the draft he'd received from Ke Li. The check was for $15,000, by far the largest deposit to date for the new bank. While Chester showed no emotion other than thanking Ben for the deposit in a very gracious fashion, he knew he would want to get to know him better over a period of time.

Ernest C. Frazier

CHAPTER 2

ESCAPE FROM ANDERSONVILLE

A company of barefooted Yankee prisoners slogged through the steaming, life-sucking muck of a snake-infested swamp. Captain Malcolm Frazier, rancher turned soldier-now a Confederate prisoner-slipped and fell to his knees. A bullwhip whistled in the air and popped a sliver of flesh off his raw and festering back. He recoiled in agony but was far too exhausted to cry out. Like a dumb animal, he pulled himself up and plodded on, trying to keep his mind active, trying to find some sane reason to continue his tortured existence. For his six months of captivity he'd been able to flood his mind with memories of his wife, Steffi, and little Hugh, their son who would be four years old. He wondered, *am I a father again?* When he last saw Steffi, she believed he would be, but, since no mail reached him, he could only wonder.

The sun dipped to touch the horizon and the starving men, steaming with sweat and caked in mud, began dragging the logs they felled that day back to their malaria-ridden camp. Andersonville, the most dreaded prison in the south, a hellhole bursting at the seams with thousands of emaciated souls, was their destination. It was there in that stinking stockade that Yankee soldiers died by the thousands from gangrene, polluted water, overwork, disease, starvation, and, suicide.

Six months earlier Malcolm had hope and constantly thought of escape. As the days wore on, he began to realize his dreams were little more than idle speculation. Every night he heard the baying of hounds and mongrels working the swamps, flushing out would be escapees and dragging them back to camp, torn half to pieces.

15

The roads, patrolled by cavalrymen, provided no avenue for escape. He could hear them yelling in the distance, riding down prisoners who made it to the road. The chases usually ended with gunfire, then, silence. Prisoners were rousted out before dawn to bury their comrades. Anyone making it to the swamps found them unforgiving, teeming with poisonous snakes, ravenous alligators, and bogs that could swallow a man or a horse in minutes. For miles around, the southern civilians were hostile and never hesitated to use a pitchfork on a Yankee hiding in their barn. Malcolm never saw a successful prisoner escape in six months. Those that tried, and lived, wished they'd never tried it.

Having lost forty pounds on a diet of collard greens, chunks of moldy bread, and watered down hominy soup, his mind seemed to be shutting down. In his delirium, he realized he was starving to death. He'd watched hundreds just like himself lay down and never rise again. He knew he would join them soon. In a tragic irony, the war would soon end but the men in Andersonville had no way of knowing that. It was 8PM on Sunday night. Heavy clouds obliterated the heavens and darkness fell in a matter of minutes. Struggling with an oversize log, Malcolm fell further behind. Soon he was a good twenty yards behind the others. His mind drifted, unfocused, and he couldn't remember where he was. His will to live was drifting away. What he didn't know was that the delay was a blessing in disguise. For now, he was just trying to keep on his feet. Mounted guards rode on each side of the prisoners, whipping and prodding those that faltered. Two guards led the procession which now strung out for two miles. Behind him, an overseer they called the Weasel, brought up the rear. A bullwhip was looped over his saddle horn. It had slashed through Malcolm's rotted shirt dozens of times that day, hundreds of times over the past six months. Right now, however, the Weasel had a greater problem than keeping track of Malcolm. His horse had hit a soft spot in the bog and was sucked into his knees. The Weasel jumped off, grabbed the reins, and flogged the animal into bucking itself free. Ahead, up on the road, an artillery regiment was thundering by with great fanfare, saluting the prison with drum rolls and bugle calls.

Malcolm saw the horse pull itself from the muck, gain a foot hold on dry ground, then rear up and fall over backward, momentarily pinning one of the Weasel's legs to the ground. The helpless man screamed for help. Malcolm's mind cleared in that instant, realizing that no one else could hear the call. *He's helpless! I've got one chance!* A charge of adrenalin ignited him to action. He dropped his log, grabbed a four-foot limb, and waded back where his tormentor, having drug himself free, was scrambling on his knees to retrieve his rifle. He didn't make it. Malcolm swung the club with all the power he could muster. The club broke over the Weasel's head. Malcolm grabbed the rifle, but one look told him he didn't need it. He pressed his finger against the man's neck. There was no pulse. In those seconds, Malcolm breathed freedom for the first time in months. He glanced ahead. Nobody was coming back. They weren't missed-yet. The marching regiment provided perfect cover with their racket. He tied the horse to a stump, stripped off the overseer's uniform, buried his own clothes in the swamp, washed up the best he could, and donned the Confederate uniform. It fit his emaciated form fairly well. The boots were two sizes too large but nobody would notice. He pushed the naked overseer into the swamp and watched while the body slid from sight. He mounted up and pushed into the swamp. He traveled at night, slipping by the numerous patrols that stayed up on the roads. During the day, he let his horse graze and slept in the woods. When he could, he took food and grain from farms along the way. He found potatoes, corn, and beans, which he boiled, and cabbages and carrots which he ate raw. On the rare occasions when he encountered Confederate soldiers, they barely gave him a second glance. Couriers were constantly delivering messages from one camp to the other and he easily passed for one of them.

It seemed like he rode forever but he crossed the Oklahoma border and entered Kansas, dressed in civilian clothes and riding

17

a fresh horse, items he'd found on a burned out Missouri farm. He was still a few miles from his ranch. Wanting Steffi to be the first one to greet him and wanting no delays, he detoured around Alexander, as everyone there knew him.

A few miles north of town, he crossed a creek, the property line that marked the beginning of the Wandering S. His spirits soared! *Only five more miles. Then, I'm home!*

He rode through a herd of cattle grazing in the pasture. He noticed the absence of yearling calves. *Maybe Steffi is having to sell some to pay on our note.*

The cattle were fat as the grass was tall and lush. He knew that Jim Stevenson, his brother-in-law, was helping Steffi with the ranch. She couldn't handle it alone. A mile later, he passed the Stevenson ranch. It sat a quarter of a mile off the road. He saw no activity and assumed that Molly, Steffi's sister, was in the house with little Petey Dinks, and Jim was either helping out at the Wandering S or was out working his own cattle. He by-passed their place and pressed on. Steffi was foremost on his mind. The sun was going to set within the hour. He wanted to get home before dark.

Steffi kept a double barrel shotgun on the mantle above the fireplace. Out in the barn, a .30 caliber Winchester hung on a peg next to the bridles and harnesses. Both guns were loaded.

Hugh and his baby brother, Colin, tagged along behind Steffi. They were going to the windmill so she could stop the pump. The watering tank was full and the wind was coming up. She figured, *No need to have water running all over the place.* As she pulled the lever to stop the flow, she saw Colin stop and sit down in a puddle full of tadpoles. "Get him out of there!" she yelled, yanking on the lever to stop the windmill. She was aggravated. The boy would need another bath. She'd just gotten him out of the tub and had thrown the hot water out. But, she was sorry she'd yelled at Hugh. It wasn't his fault. She gripped her head with both hands. *My nerves are shot. I don't know if the boys have a father or not, whether he's dead or alive. Jim is neglecting his own family to help us out, we're in debt and I don't know how much longer I can handle all this!*

"You boys follow me," she ordered and walked over to the clothesline. A week's supply of laundry had been hanging there all day. She reached up to grab a shirt and a movement on the horizon caught her attention. A horseman, almost a mile away crested a hill. She watched with idle curiosity and continued pulling clothes off the line. He surprised her by suddenly spurring his horse to a gallop. She realized, *He's riding right toward our place!*

"Hugh! Run get Mama the spyglass! Bring it to the barn! Run!"

Hugh took off as fast as his stubby legs would carry him. She grabbed Colin, ran into the barn, deposited him in a stall full of hay, and grabbed the Winchester. She'd heard stories about what happened to pioneer women trapped far from town without a husband. It wasn't going to happen to her and her boys.

The rider was closing fast. Hugh ran back with the spyglass. Colin was shrieking to get out but no one was listening. Steffi steadied the glass against the barn door. The horseman had on a farmer's straw hat and overalls, but something about the way he rode captured her attention. Her eyes widened and her mouth fell open. *It's him!* She dropped the spyglass, picked up Colin who had escaped from the stall, and, with Hugh in hot pursuit, ran from the barn screaming, "Your daddy is coming home!"

Malcolm jumped off the horse as it slid to a stop, threw the hat twenty yards in the air, and grabbed Steffi and the boys up in his arms.

The evening was spent with the boys crawling all over their daddy while Steffi cooked supper. She decided that the clothes on the line could hang there all night. She couldn't keep her eyes off her husband. *He's a lot thinner. He's quieter. He's got a harder look in his eyes.* He told her he'd been in prison for six months and that he'd killed a guard to escape. That was the extent of his discussion about the war. He changed the subject. She could tell, by his silence, that he'd suffered greatly.

The boys finally calmed down enough to play with a couple

of toys on the floor. Steffi settled down on the sofa next to Malcolm. He drew her into his arms and held her tight. Needing to get reacquainted, they talked for a long time about the boys, the town, Jim and Molly, everything but the war.

It was getting late.

"Jim and I rounded up thirty yearlings to sell," Steffi said. "Chester's not worrying about our note but you know me. I don't like debt. Maybe we can pay most of it off this year."

"I figured as much. I came in through the south pasture. Probably a good idea. 'Course, I'm a Scotsman. You know I hate paying interest."

She asked if he came through town and if he'd talked to anyone they knew.

"Honey, I decided you were going to be the first person here to see me. I didn't stop anywhere!" He kissed her softly and tugged at her ear lobe.

Steffi glanced at his eyes. They'd softened. The old sparkle was back. She smiled, "Do you suppose it's time we took the boys up to bed?"

"I think so."

Later, as he tossed and turned in his sleep, Steffi's fingers found the ridges of scar tissue on his back. She cried softly for the rest of the night, imagining the horrible treatment he'd experienced, fearing how those scars, and his emotional scars, could change their lives.

In the morning, they hitched up the buckboard and rode over to see Jim and Molly. They'd been worried sick about Steffi and the boys ever since Malcolm left. Now, a great burden was lifted from all of them. After a morning of non-stop conversation and a dinner of roast chicken, Malcolm loaded his family back in the buckboard.

"One more thing," Jim said, innocently announcing some local news. "Times are changin'. I hear that a family of Chinese are movin' to town."

"Why would they come here?" Malcolm asked. "There's never been any in this part of the world."

"I don't know. Rumor is they may take over the hotel restaurant. I reckon we'll find out soon enough. But it is strange."

"Interesting," Malcolm said. "I never met anyone from China before."

Then they rode back home.

Ernest C. Frazier

CHAPTER 3

THE BANKER

Chester Zimmerman walked into the bank, nodded a crisp greeting to his employees, stepped into his office and shut the door. He saw the jar full of white powder sitting on his desk and was relieved. It'd come by train from his father-in-law in Indiana. He took a tin cup from a file cabinet, filled it from his water pitcher, mixed in the powder, and drained it in a few gulps. The nagging ache in his stomach subsided.

He opened his mail; blissfully ignorant of the approaching role his ailment would play in fusing together the families of Ben Wang, his newest customer, and Malcolm Frazier, the rancher. For now, Chester was well pleased. He and his wife had moved to Alexander less than a year ago and were already accepted members of the community.

Two years earlier, in Terra Haute, Indiana, the social news of the year was to be Chester's marriage, to Edna Brown, the doctor's daughter. The marriage of the forty-year-old son of a wealthy banker and the old maid schoolteacher, unfortunately, drew little attention. For a year or so, Edna, craving recognition, worked her heart out to become a leading matron of Terra Haute society. Her success was very limited. Sick to death of working in his father's bank and the failure of social recognition, they seized the opportunity to move to the frontier town of Alexander, a town in dire need of a bank. It appeared to be a smart move, one, which by the very nature of Chester's position of bank president, would bestow on them the social position they craved. It sounded like a foolproof plan. But Edna's gnawing desire for social gain was to have devastating results.

Chester's parents had loaned him a small amount of start up capital. They were aware that, out west, the government had granted millions of acres of land to the railroads in return of their promise to build tracks to the west coast. The railroads

23

granted land along the right-of-way to settlers. That, along with the Homestead Act, made it possible for common people to become landowners. Thousands of families rushed west. The crops and livestock they raised would provide the freight needed for the railroads to become profitable.

The new settlers were in need of investment capital. Chester knew that a frontier banker could not only expect success, but could become wealthy if he played his cards right. Also, he had to keep his wife happy. Edna would create a genteel society for the ladies in the area, many who had never drunk tea off fine china or been exposed to a hand of bridge. Her mother was the uncrowned queen of Terra Haute society and Edna wanted that same role in Alexander.

Chester's funds were limited so he had to find local people in the area to buy stock and serve on the board of his new bank.

Looking around the boomtown, he assumed that investors wouldn't be hard to find.

He talked to Eric Binford who'd recently built a new livery stable. He would have gladly served on the board but had no money to invest.

Across the street, Angus McDougal, nicknamed Iron Man Mac, ran his blacksmith shop. Chester heard he was the strongest, and, biggest man in the county. Many a cowboy had tried to put him down in arm wrestling. No one ever lasted more than five seconds with McDougal. Angus McDougal was strong, but he too was strapped for cash.

Next door, the Goodnite Inn was in operation. It sported a well equipped restaurant which needed someone to operate it. Chester knew that Jack Goodnite had money and would be a valuable addition to the board.

Shorty the barber, with the help of an orphan boy, Raymond Crocker, ran the Inn's barber shop. Haircuts were 35 cents, shaves 25 cents and bath's 40 cents, not enough to provide Shorty with any investment dollars.

Harold Fry operated the only mortuary in the area. No one knew much about Harold except that he was a shy bachelor.

Morticians were hard to find so even one named Fry could expect plenty of business. A recent out break of deadly flu had boosted profits. Harold had money but Chester couldn't see him serving on the board because he wouldn't offer any opinions.

J. T. Smith was a good candidate. He'd made money in Missouri in his general store that outfitted settlers, miners, cowboys, and other adventurers but was looking for excitement. After hearing of the fantastic opportunities in the new boomtown, they gave the store to their son, J. T., Jr., and moved to Alexander.

Business was great, even though a lot of it was on credit. For household goods, the settlers had been depending on wandering peddlers who hawked their wares door to door offering everything from bar soap to Persian rugs.

They brought one employee, Moses Farmer, a freed slave, to do the heavy work. Except for a few harmless, practical jokes, the community accepted him as one of their own.

Ranchers Jesse Monts and George Norton were big in cattle. They agreed to invest along with Smith, Goodnite, and Chester and Edna. Chester, still short of capital, needed one final stockholder to make a major investment. No one came forward. His fellow directors offered a solution: Ben Wang. They believed he was wealthy and had money to invest.

Chester wasn't enthused about asking an Oriental to serve on his prestigious board. He knew that Chinese businessmen were industrious almost to a fault, financed each other's business ventures without charging interest, and saved far more money than their Anglo neighbors. While those attributes were to be admired, he worried about the bank's image, *A Chinaman on the board?* His position softened when he heard of two Italian coal miners who founded a bank in Missouri that was doing quite well. *Maybe 'foreigners' are becoming acceptable,* he reasoned. Ben certainly met the two most important criteria: Money and a mind for business. With that in mind he asked his new depositor in for a talk.

Ernest C. Frazier

CHAPTER 4

SMOOTH MOUTH SAM

Smooth Mouth would ride south into New Mexico territory, turn west to the Navajo country of Arizona, then back south to the Mexican border. The Navajo were at peace so he had nothing to fear and he looked forward to the trip. The Canyon de Chelly and Monument Valley areas, home to the tribes, consisted of spectacular rock formations, cliff dwellings, and flat topped mesas that offered a feast for the eyes.

His mine was located on the Arizona-Mexico border. Levi and Hitch, the twins he raised after their mother's death, were all the help he needed. They worked the mine alone, not trusting other miners and prospectors who might become claim jumpers upon hearing of a strike. It was well known that a miner hitting a rich vein could be wealthy in the morning but dead that night. Smooth Mouth and his boys were looking for silver but kept unearthing copper, a metal with little use as far as they knew.

Outside of Durango, he stopped to adjust his load and caught a glimpse of two riders following a mile or so behind. They soon dropped out of view, and, unconcerned, he rode on. That night he camped on top of a mesa. Down in the valley he saw a fire flickering and wondered if it came from the camp of the same two riders. .

He didn't see them the next morning. A few days later he entered Arizona territory and turned south. The riders were nowhere to be seen so he forgot them. The Navajo country was a forbidding land of sand, rocks, and cactus, reminiscent of the great deserts of Asia. He marveled at how the Navajo survived the brutal environment. The few he encountered paid him little attention. He was not a novelty as prospectors constantly visited the area.

Days later, he entered the high country. Cactus and sand gave way to scrub oak, juniper, and, higher up, tall pines. He stopped a few miles outside of Holbrook. Worn out, he pitched camp. He would rest a day or two before going into town. In the morning he fixed his standard breakfast of biscuits, gravy, and salt pork. He was pouring his first cup of coffee when caught a glimpse of two riders approaching. His hand shook, spilling his coffee. *They might be the riders that followed me out of Durango.*

He poked uneasily at his fire. As they approached, he saw that they were Chinese.

Smooth Mouth displayed no weapon, but he was no fool. Secure in his boot was his .44 that could drop an elk, or a man, at forty paces.

"Howdy," he said. "You fellows lookin' for somethin'?"

"We may be on the wrong trail," the taller of the two replied in good English. "We are going to California. Do you know where the trail turns west?"

"We're about five miles north of Holbrook. When you get there you take the main trail west to Flagstaff and on in to California," Smooth Mouth was glad to offer directions hoping to send them on their way.

"We haven't eaten for two days," the tall one spoke again. "We will pay you for food."

"I guess there ain't no harm in that," Smooth Mouth offered, warming to the idea of having some company for a while. Also he could satisfy his curiosity. He wondered just why they left Durango at the same time he did and, incredibly, turned up now, hundreds of miles away, at his campground.

"Sure, set down. I'll throw on some more biscuits and gravy. Two bits is all you owe me for the food. You can hobble your horses with my mules in the meadow." Smooth Mouth was suddenly now the gracious host, hopefully making his guests comfortable and talkative.

It remained chilly after breakfast. Smooth Mouth took a deep snort from a jug he kept for 'medicinal purposes' and

28

offered his guests a drink. Gratefully, they accepted. Soon their tongues loosened and one of them asked, "Where are the Chinese man and woman who are traveling with you?"

"I don't know what the devil you're talkin' about," Smooth Mouth answered, agitated as he began to understand why he'd been followed. "The only Chinese I know are Ben Wang and his wife that I met in Durango. They left town at the same time I did but they had their own rig and headed east. Maybe they were going to Kansas or clear on to St. Joe. There's some Chinese there "

"That is strange. The man who runs the hotel said you all left together in one wagon," the tall one, looking straight into Smooth Mouth's eyes, spoke with remarkable clarity, causing Smooth Mouth to squirm a bit under his stare.

"Well, he don't know nothin' about it. He must of heard us at supper when we said we'd all be leavin' the next day. But no one said we were leavin' together and any fool can look at my wagon and see it's just me and my mules. Why are you wantin' to know about them anyway? You could have looked 'em up in Durango."

Again, it was the tall one who answered, "We only heard that Ben Wang was in Durango but we did not know where to find him. We have business with him from our days in China. It is only by accident that we happened to be returning to California at this time and you were on the same trail."

Smooth Mouth tensed, knowing he was being lied to. He wondered, *Why'd they wait 'till I was clear out in Arizona before they showed up with this cock-and-bull story? They could've caught me anytime. This don't make no sense a'tall.*

Stalling for time, he responded, "Well, I don't know nothin' about it. There's lots of places they could go to." He shifted his eyes away from the unnerving stare of his interrogator.

The tall one opened a purse full of gold coins, counted out a hundred dollars worth and said, "We have great need to find out where they are going. As you can see, I am willing to pay for that information."

Smooth Mouth saw it was the equivalent of several months' wages for a workingman, but alarm bells were ringing in his head. He believed that he would be signing Ben and Su Chang's death warrants if he told of their plans.

He decided to bluff and replied, "You can keep your money. I don't have the foggiest notion where those people went. They might have headed north to Wyoming for all I know."

His bluff failed.

"You lie! You know where they went. Tell us now or your life is worth nothing!" He grabbed Smooth Mouth's hair and shoved the point of a dagger against his adam's apple. Smooth Mouth jerked back, clawing for his boot top and the hard hickory handle of his pistol. He yanked the gun out and fired as a chopping blow shattered his wrist. The bullet flew wild and the weapon fell to the ground.

Then they drug him to his wagon, brutally spread eagled him and tied him to one of the wheels.

The short man commanded, "Tell us now where Ben Wang and his wife were going!"

Smooth Mouth spit at him, "There ain't no way I'll tell you anything!" he yelled, then gasped and jerked violently as a riding crop, wielded by the short man, popped skin from his back.

The question was repeated. Smooth Mouth did not answer so he felt the lash again, at least fifteen times. He ground his teeth. His vision blurred as his body sagged under the whip. But, still, he would not speak.

"Let him rest," the tall one spoke, "don't let him lose consciousness. I'll heat the branding iron. "He'll talk."

They waited until the iron burned red and radiated heat waves. Then they took it from the fire. Smooth Mouth strained against his bonds, his heart pounding out of control. He was gripped with fear, an unreasonable fear, the type that only a man facing death or torture can understand. He considered revealing what he knew of Ben's plans, but down in his heart, he knew he would die even if he gave the information. He already knew too much. He decided to keep his mouth shut.

He almost swooned as he felt the heat close to his back. His protruding, bloodshot eyes searched the countryside for any sign of help. He gave up all hope, mumbling out a plea for mercy along with a silent prayer. Then he saw what he thought was a vision. As though on command, three cowboys driving a small herd of steers came into view.

"Hey, what are you doin'?" the closest cowboy, about twenty yards away, hollered. He and his two partners drew their weapons, shocked by the sight of two 'foreigners' preparing to brand a man tied to a wagon wheel!

There was no response from the 'foreigners', one of which was already applying the brand.

A scream welled up then died in Smooth Mouth's throat. He passed out instantly. The iron, shaped as a small hand, sizzled and popped against his flesh, scoring deep into his shoulder. The last thing he heard was gunfire.

Five minutes passed before the cowboys could revive him. They used his lard and axle grease to dress the burn and tied a rag around his swollen wrist. Next to campfire was the body of one of his assailants, shot through the head with one shot from a .44.

"What happened to the other one?" Smooth Mouth inquired.

"Dunno. He jumped down that ravine the minute we yelled and we never could find 'im. He plumb got away. Jim plugged this one just as he was layin' the brand on your hide," the cowboy wearing chaps spoke. "Jist why was those Chinamen out here tryin' to brand you, anyway? We never seen any of them around here before. It's a strange brand. They branded you with the mark of a hand. We know all the ranches around here and ain't none of them have a brand like that."

These were questions that Smooth Mouth was asking himself. He explained his chance meeting with Ben and Su Chang, and that they were going to Kansas but hadn't revealed their past to him. He told them they might be going to Alexander. He explained, "Looks to me like they were running from these gangsters," he said.

"We'll harness your mules and take you into Holbrook. Tomorrow is Tuesday and a circuit doctor will be in town. Get him to treat your burn and that busted wrist. You could get blood poisoning. Also, we need to report all this to the sheriff. We'll use your wagon to haul the dead Chinaman in and he can decide what to do with him." Once again it was the cowboy in chaps who did the talking.

In Holbrook the sheriff and coroner examined the corpse. They'd never seen an Oriental before but the sheriff was aware of their presence in California and Colorado.

"You said they started trackin' you outside of Durango?" the sheriff asked. Without waiting for a reply, he continued, "What we've got here is a member of the Black Hand Society. The brand on your shoulder is a dead give-away. My brother-in-law is a marshal in Monterey and he told me all about the secret societies. They're sendin' people to Colorado to try to get a foothold in the opium, gambling and girlie businesses there. They're minin' coal up there and some gold and silver so there's lots of money around. These Chinamen must have had it in for Ben Wang. He probably didn't know the Tong was active in Durango. Maybe he beat 'em in some business deal or wouldn't pay protection money-they're big in that racket-so they decided to hunt him down. You just happened to get in the way."

Smooth Mouth spent two weeks recuperating in Holbrook. He had another month of travel before he would get to his mine.

"Any news about the Chinaman that got away?" he asked the sheriff before he left.

"No, and we may never find him. There's nothin' but wilderness country clear from here to California, if that's where he went. Even our Indian trackers ain't found a trace of the man."

CHAPTER 5

THE INVITATION

Ben's curiosity was aroused when he received a note from his banker asking him to a meeting. He'd heard that Chester was having trouble filling the last seat on the board but he assumed the meeting would not be about that. He knew he didn't have any banking problem. He'd made many deposits, owed no money, and the restaurant was doing well. As the only first class restaurant for miles around, it was becoming the social hub of the community.

Ben waited while Chester finalized his business with one of the local ranchers. When he was done he came out to the waiting room, put his arm around Ben's shoulders and said, "Let's go into my office. I've got a proposition for you."

"As you know," Chester began, "the bank board has been operating one man short. You are fairly new in town but you've proven you can run a business and the people here like you. We think you would be a great addition to the board. We'd like you to come to our monthly meeting next Wednesday and discuss the possibility of your joining the board. If you agree to come, and I hope you won't let us down, I'll pick you up in my buckboard after supper on Wednesday and we'll go in together."

Ben scarcely believed his ears. Here was the banker, the most prominent citizen in town, asking him, an Oriental, to consider an appointment to the board of directors-a board which traditionally would be 100% Caucasian. He knew that prejudice wasn't a big thing in Alexander. It was just the way things were done, or, not done. He concluded that money must be the issue. He wondered how much additional capital they needed, but he didn't ask. It could wait until Wednesday.

"Of course, I would be pleased to be considered as a member of your board. It would be a great honor to attain such a position."

Chester pumped his hand again, this time barely suppressing his glee. After some small talk, he escorted Ben to the door, reminding him that he'd pick him up Wednesday night.

That night, Ben told Su Chang of the invitation and showed her a copy of the bank's Statement of Condition he'd brought home to study. It detailed the fact that the bank was to be capitalized by the purchase of 100,000 shares of stock at a par value of $1.00 per share. To date, 70,000 shares had been sold leaving 30,000 available.

"Chester only needs one more stockholder," Ben pointed out, "but if he sells me all 30,000 shares I will become the largest single stockholder in the bank. He has 15, 000 shares in his name and Mrs. Zimmerman has 15,000. They are in good shape only if they vote together on all issues. If he has thought this through, he would not want to sell me 30,000 shares, individually. As an individual, I would be the major shareholder. Because of those considerations, he may want to only offer me 15,000 shares or less and bring on someone else to purchase the balance."

Su Chang pondered Ben's comments and, as she spoke, Ben could see that she understood the logic in his explanation, "You are telling me that under certain conditions you could control the bank, or at least bank policy, with a thirty thousand dollar stock purchase. What rights would you have on the board if you purchased a lesser amount?"

"None, a minority shareholder has no power. Others on the board either don't understand that or they don't care. Maybe they just want the prestige of serving on the banks' board of directors.

"So, what do you intend to do?"

"Chester is running out of time. I've heard he has less than ten days to raise the money. But, I do not want to be in a minority position. My plan is simple. I will attend the meeting and offer to buy the entire $30,000 worth. If they accept, I will give them my promissory note and telegraph Ke Li. He will sell our valuables and wire us the proceeds. There will be more than enough to cover the note."

Ben's introduction to the board was met with a great deal of interest. The members knew Ben from their visits to his restaurant. Other than that, they knew nothing of his business experience or qualifications to set on the board. They were ranchers and small town businessmen who understood cattle and the retail business but were very ignorant of banking procedures. They were impressed when Ben told them of his past experiences in China in the silk trade. He explained he'd learned the business from the silkworm's creative process all the way through the distribution of the finished product. He told them of Su Chang's apprenticeship in the kitchens of Ke Li, training they now put to use in their own restaurant. Chester was absolutely mesmerized by his report.

"Ben," he asked, "we have 30,000 shares of stock for sale at $1.00 per share. If we extend the opportunity of board membership to you, how many shares are you willing to purchase?"

"Gentlemen," Ben addressed the entire group, "I am a foreigner in your midst but it is my desire, and my wife's desire to become good citizens and contribute to the community. We can think of no better way to accomplish that than by providing assurance that the bank obtains the capital it needs. Therefore, I am prepared to provide the balance you require by individually purchasing the 30,000 shares that are for sale."

As he spoke, he carefully observed the expression on Chester's face. A frown would mean that Chester didn't like the implications of that purchase. A smile would mean that he wasn't overly concerned about the voting rights issue, and would recommend that the board accept Ben's offer.

Chester smiled. Ben was relieved. There would be no unpleasantries, no discussion of voting rights. He knew his offer would be accepted.

Ben adjourned to the lobby while his proposal was taken under consideration. Soon he was called back in to receive a formal offer of board membership--an offer he accepted with gracious dignity.

CHAPTER 6

DAO CHI

Dao Chi had just handed the branding iron to Mi Qing when the three cowboys rode up. At the sound of gunfire, he dove headlong over the side of a steep cliff. Heavy brush broke his fall, saving his life. Unchecked, he would have fallen several hundred feet. He knew the cowboys couldn't follow him on horseback and he had an excellent chance to escape in the undergrowth. He left Mi Qing--unaware he was already dead--to fend for himself.

Dao Chi and Mi Qing had been dispatched by Kai Mang, the powerful tong chief in California with orders to kidnap Su Chang, hide her in Durango to shake off any pursuers, then bring her to San Francisco. She would become part of his household of lovely, Oriental women. Kai Mang was fat and aging but he remembered the beautiful Su Chang as a young girl in China. She had served him and his retinue years earlier when they visited the compound of Ke Li. While in China, Kai Mang had purchased several beautiful girls from impoverished families for transport back to California. Su Chang was not for sale then, but now, with the changing tides of fortune, she was within his reach--if only his men could find her. Her capture would punish Ben for his insult against the tong, and, more importantly, would send a loud signal throughout the community: "Cooperate without question when given an order by the tong. Failure to do so is never forgiven. Look at the example of Su Chang."

Capturing Ben was not part of the plan. He was to die. However, if he escaped, his punishment would be inflicted daily by the knowledge that his beautiful wife was the possession of another.

Dao Chi had no intention of returning to Durango without

Su Chang as his failure would seal his fate. So even though they had made a bad error in judgment in trailing Smooth Mouth Sam, he was determined to backtrack to Durango and see if he couldn't pick up Ben and Su Chang's trail from there. *The cowboys and the old prospector think I'm fleeing to California. They won't suspect that I might return to Durango.*

He guessed right. The posse from Holbrook headed straight west.

He hadn't been able to retrieve his horse so he started out on foot. He found water in small creeks but no large game. Fortunately he could throw his dagger with uncanny accuracy. In the evening when the mountain squirrels frolicked in the trees around him, he would quietly lay out a large stash of pinon nuts. Hunger and curiosity created an irresistible combination and soon one of them would come within range. He kept alive on squirrel meat until he spotted a small herd of deer. Being miles from the nearest ranch, he shot one with his pistol. He dressed the animal, cooked all he could eat, then cured a large portion with salt he'd found in a line shack. The deerskin provided him with hide for moccasins and a smelly blanket. Not wanting want to draw attention to himself, he avoided everyone, exiting the trail far in advance of any oncoming travelers.

Weeks later he arrived back in Durango, dusted with the flakes of the first winter snow. He made a lot of inquiries and heard that Ben and Su Chang had probably fled to Alexander, Kansas. He now felt secure enough to purchase a pony and provisions from a rancher. Seeing that Dao Chi was familiar with livestock, the rancher offered him a job with room and board, clothing, and a small wage.

"No one can work calves dressed in pajamas and wearing a little box hat. I'll have Marge cut off that top not off your head. Ain't no one working for me going to have hair braided like that!" the rancher declared.

That comment hit Dao Chi as a slap in the face. His queue was his symbol of manhood. He hated the whites who looked down on his people as ignorant coolies. But, he was a survivor.

His duty was to survive and fulfill his mission.

He smiled graciously. "Winter snows are upon us and I have no where else to go. I will be pleased to work throughout the winter. I accept your generous offer." He wondered if he should kill the rancher and his wife. *It would only take a quick thrust of his dagger.* The thought amused him as he shook hands with his new employer. *How stupid these people are.*

There was a 'looking glass' in the bunkhouse and Dao Chi saw that after his haircut and his outfit changed, he looked remarkable 'American'. He was especially pleased with the black leather chaps and hat. Most cowboys wore buckskin outfits and he liked the idea that his clothes set him apart from the rest. He was broad shouldered and stocky and his features only hinted of his Oriental background. His skin was pale, much lighter than most of his countrymen. With a little eye make up, he could pass for an Anglo, maybe a 'breed', but a far cry from the 'Chinaman in pajamas' look. The disguise would fit into his master plan. The abduction of Su Chang would be carried out by an 'American Cowboy', not a poor Chinese coolie.

Ernest C. Frazier

CHAPTER 7

STEFFI AND SU CHANG

It was inevitable that Steffi and Su Chang would meet in Alexander and it was natural that the women would be drawn to each other. Both were beauties, each in her own right. Su Chang was much taller than most Chinese women. She possessed a classic 'China Doll' complexion with her coal black hair providing a striking contrast to her porcelain like features. She wore it piled high on her head, the acceptable style in her homeland. Her wardrobe was varied and in exquisite taste. As hostess in her own restaurant, she could wear a different dress, (all beautiful silks), night after night, as she moved among her guests, engaging them in light hearted conversation while being ever attentive to their needs. Local ladies, mature women--some never married, some widowed by the recent war--worked under her watchful eye to become first-rate waitresses. Others were supervised by Ben in the kitchen. They were quickly transformed from women simply handy with a frying pan, into skilled cooks, skills sadly lacking in the western territories.

Steffi offered the complete contrast to Su Chang. She was slightly shorter but had a matching figure. Childbirth had not diminished her in any way and she moved with an air of self-confidence, far more so than most of the rancher's wives. But, it was natural, it was 'Steffi', and her radiant personality won her not only acceptance but also a certain amount of envy. She could change roles from the rancher's wife in boot pants (her standard outfit), to the sophisticated lady, dressed up, dining in town and charming everyone in the place. A lot of the boys, and some of the women around town called her a 'high stepper', sort of a back-handed compliment describing a self contained woman who knows who she is, what she wants, and where she is going.

41

Even the Methodist preacher turned his head when Steffi walked by, and everyone knew it.

Su Chang, thrilled to have a new friend, told Steffi all about her life in China.

Steffi wanted to involve her in the town's social activities so she asked Edna Zimmerman about the possibilities. Edna was a bit of a snob but in this case she thought it would be a splendid idea, especially since Ben was a major stockholder in their bank. "We can ask her to serve on the committee for Beth's baby shower. She might enjoy that. We could approach her about that. Why don't you ask if we could see her on Friday."

Steffi stopped in the restaurant and told Su Chang what they were thinking about. Su Chang was delighted. "A few months ago I had no time to engage in social activities as we were so busy getting the restaurant going. But, now a year has passed, and I do need some social diversion."

They arranged to meet at 3PM on Friday.

Some distance to the east, a lone cowboy in black chaps and hat, stopped at a rancher's house to water his horse and ask directions. "How far is it to Alexander?"

"About forty miles," was the reply.

"I should get in there on Friday," the rider spoke as he slowly rode away leaving the rancher to wonder, *Who's this odd lookin' cowboy? What business would he have in Alexander?*

CHAPTER 8

THE TONG ARRIVES

When Dao Chi rode into Alexander at daybreak, the Goodnite Inn appeared to be the only place open for business. A young boy, probably thirteen or so, sat alone on the veranda. Dao Chi pulled up and asked if he knew of Ben and Su Chang.

"Sure," Raymond Crocker replied. "Everyone knows 'em. They run the restaurant here. Ben's gone to Medicine Lodge for supplies but his wife is here. They live upstairs. In fact, I take her hot water from the barbershop. She makes tea and stuff in her room. Do you want me to go see if she's up?"

"I may want to call later in the day. It would be a more respectable hour to visit. What is their room number?"

Raymond paused for a moment, then decided it couldn't do any harm to talk to the man. He seemed pretty decent and the boy was lonely. Not too many adults asked him about anything.

"Room 1- A. First one at the top of the stairs. Only suite with two rooms. Only one that opens out the back. Has a 'widows walk', kind of an upstairs porch out over the back patio. Ain't no other hotel in Kansas built like that" Raymond elaborated, eager to please and watching for acceptance in the eye of the mysterious stranger.

Dao Chi nodded and flipped him an Indian head nickel. Raymond snatched it from the air and exclaimed, "Gosh, thanks a lot!" The stranger nodded again, then rode away. Raymond shoved the nickel into his overalls, entered the barbershop, pitched some wood in the stove, and started heating water.

Dao Chi was pleased with what he'd just heard. He rode around town, making a mental note of the streets and buildings. In particular, Harold Fry's mortuary with its' inventory of new caskets caught his attention. *Very good*, he thought, sensing a unique opportunity. *Very good*. He knew that abducting Su Chang would be extremely dangerous. Men were hanged for stealing horses so he could imagine his fate if he were captured kidnapping a human being. He knew that her husband was gone, probably for the day, eliminating any threat from him. Dao Chi had come to town without any real plan of attack. But, the caskets would solve his problem. He turned his horse around and rode two blocks to the railway station. Cletus Morgan, the depot agent, was glad to answer his questions about the train schedules.

"Two trains stop here everyday, one goin' east and one goin' west," Cletus explained. "Number 67 comes in here at 3:30 in the afternoon. She takes on coal and water then goes to Springfield, Missouri. She pulls out of here at 4:55.

Number 88, heading west to Colorado, comes in at 4:00 and is switched over to the siding. She leaves later, at 5:15. Both trains haul passengers and freight."

"Good, that fits into my plans," said Dao Chi. "A lady is traveling with me. We're going to St. Louis." He bought two tickets to St. Louis via Springfield.

"Also," he continued, "an old friend of mine was visiting here and died two days ago. The mortuary embalmed her body and it's to be shipped to her family in Durango, Colorado. I cannot accompany the casket since I'm going to St. Louis, but, a young man who worked for her family is here to do that. Tell me, what would it cost for him to ride in the freight car with the casket and body?"

Cletus shoved his visor back on his head, stretched his suspenders and took a good look at Dao Chi. *Who is this hombre, anyway? He don't talk or look like most of the people around her. Probably from back east. Lots of strange people live back there.* But, Cletus wasn't paid to worry about it. His job was to run the station, not to figure out the variety of characters passing through. He let his curiosity rest and replied, "Well, the only people that ride in the freight car are usually takin' care of an animal. Riding back there costs one-fourth the price of a passenger ticket. I can tell you it's a long ride and he'd better take some food and water. We only open up that car in towns where we are takin' on freight."

Dao Chi readily agreed to the costs, paid the agent, and went back to town.

Cletus still wondered where the lady was that Dao Chi bought a ticket for and the whereabouts of the other passenger that was going to accompany the casket. His attention was soon diverted. The telegraph key began its monotonous clattering. Another message was coming in for J. T. Smith. *Probably from prospectors he grubstaked,* Cletus thought as he scribbled down the message. *They always need more time or more credit.* He saw this was from an old sourdough who seemed to know Ben Wang, but it didn't make much sense. He looked outside. Two boys were rolling hoops along the tracks. He hollered, "Hey, who wants to deliver this to J. T.?"

Three minutes later, J. T. got the message, paid the boys a dime, and read: NO GOLD-STOP-COPPER TRACES-STOP-TELL BEN WANG TO BEWARE TONG-STOP. Signed: Smooth Mouth Sam

J. T. couldn't figure it out. He counted the words. Smooth Mouth had limited the message to 10 words to obtain the cheapest rate. But, the last statement meant nothing. Must have been a misspelling. J. T. had never heard of a 'Tong' but he figured that Ben would know what it was about. He would have Moses Farmer take it over to the restaurant.

When Dao Chi left the depot, he rode up to the mortuary. Harold was surprised to see a caller so early, but, as a mortician, he knew that death could come at anytime. He assumed that the cowboy was coming in to arrange a funeral.

Dao Chi explained, "Nobody has died. I only want to buy a casket and have it shipped to Durango. My mother lives there. She is old and quite ill at this time. She wants to be buried in a beautiful white casket lined with rose satin and cedar. I was happy to see that you have two of them for sale."

"Actually, one is sold and will leave here today, but I've got this one left." Harold was delighted to be getting rid of the expensive, garish caskets. They were far too fancy for the common people around Alexander. He was doubly delighted when, without questioning the price, the buyer counted out two $50 gold pieces, payment in full.

"I'll see to it that it's on the train this afternoon. Have you advised the depot agent of the destination?" Harold, ever the one for details, wanted to make sure there were no problems.

"Yes, he knows it is going to the station at Durango."

Dao Chi's next stop was the mercantile store. He bought two empty buckets, two one gallon jugs, a slab of beef jerky, hard tack biscuits, a crock of honey, a sack of dried fruit, several feet of clothesline rope, a lariat, a checkered flannel shirt, a pair of canvas trousers, a tan, military style campaign hat, a pocketknife, and a hay hook. He completed his purchases by asking J. T. for a small bottle of chloroform, the kind that ranchers used in doctoring their cattle and asked him to fill the jugs with water. J. T. accepted payment for the supplies and sent Moses to fill the jugs.

"Are you just moving into town?" J. T. asked, anxious to be friendly but a bit nosy as is customary with small town merchants.

"No, I just stopped here to make these purchases. A friend and I are taking the train on to St. Louis." Dao Chi was careful to be pleasant and asked, "I see you deal in all kinds of goods. I have a mare and saddle I need to sell before I leave. Do you deal in horses?"

"Not normally 'cause I don't have a place to stable them and Binford charges too much to board 'em. But, I might take a look at your critter. You can't afford to haul a horse on the train. Maybe we can work something out."

Dao Chi knew the animal was worth at least seventy-five dollars and the saddle, though well worn, should bring another twenty. He sensed that J. T. was a sharp trader, aware that he was under pressure to dispose of the horse. He wasn't a bit surprised when, after much hemming and hawing, J. T. finally said, "Well, I don't know how bad I need her, but I guess I'd offer forty five, cash, if you'd throw in the saddle."

46

"Can you go fifty?" Dao Chi countered, knowing he had little time to dicker.

J. T. paused, looked hard at Dao Chi, then, suppressing a slight smile, spoke one word. "Done." He opened his cash drawer and handed Dao Chi a fifty dollar gold piece.

Moses came back in with the water jugs and they led the horse out back.

J. T. asked, "Do you need some help with all that stuff? You don't have a horse now," he chuckled.

"Yes, could you spare your man for a few minutes? I need to haul it to the depot."

"Sure", J. T. grinned. "Glad to help. Moses, load this fellow in the buckboard and haul him down there. Charge him a quarter."

It was a short ride. Dao Chi asked Moses to wait while he deposited some of the supplies in the waiting room. He kept the ropes, chloroform and hay hook, and carried them back on the buckboard. He paid his quarter and was let off at the Goodnite Inn.

The veranda was deserted and he slipped inside. Seated in the foyer with her back to him was Su Chang. He knew it had to be her. There were no other Chinese women in the area. *Certainly none as lovely as her,* he thought, catching her reflection in a mirror on the wall. *Too bad that Kai Mang demands this woman for his own household. A place could be found for her in Durango.* His concentration was broken by a movement at the top of the stairs. It was Raymond Crocker pushing a tea service cart. He stopped, unlocked apartment 1-A and wheeled the cart inside. A moment later he reappeared with the cart, now empty.

Phantomlike, Dao Chi slid out a side door to the alley. He found himself standing under the apartment with the 'widow's' walk. He knew that water only stays hot for a short time. He would have only a few seconds to get into the empty apartment before Su Chang went up for her tea!

He tied the hay hook to one end of his lariat and threw it up over the wooden railing. It hooked on his first try. He pulled himself up, retrieved the rope, slid open a window, and let himself in. Su Chang was not there. His next task was to conceal himself. She would surely scream at the sight of his presence.

The clock on the mantle showed 2:50.

CHAPTER 9

THE ABDUCTION

Steffi left a note for Malcolm reminding him of her 3 PM meeting, telling him she would leave Colin and Hugh with Molly and pick them up on the way home. She harnessed one of the older mares to the buckboard and loaded the boys in the seat beside her. An hour later they were at Molly's place.

They had a brief chat. She told Molly she'd fill her in on the meeting when she came back, girl talk so necessary to the lonely rancher's wives.

Edna Zimmerman left her home at 2:45 and walked the two blocks to the Inn. Steffi was already there, tying up at the hitching post. Su Chang came out and greeted them warmly.

They chatted for a minute or two, went inside and climbed the stairs to Su Chang's apartment .

The women were visibly impressed with the decor. It was exquisitely decorated in Oriental furnishings that Ben had shipped in from California. A bone china tea service and hot water were waiting as, indeed, Raymond Crocker had been there.

Su Chang served small date cookies with their tea.

The door to the bedroom adjacent to the parlor was left ajar. Dao Chi, lying flat on his stomach under the bed, raised the bedspread ever so slightly. He had a clear view of the parlor and could hear the women talking. He pulled his watch out of his pocket and cursed softly under his breath. Time was passing. He felt a twinge of panic. It was difficult enough to deal with one woman. He could not kidnap three. The opportunity to escape with Su Chang was evaporating. His only hope was that the meeting would be short and the other women would leave.

The ladies talked on. At 3:30 a train whistled signaling the

49

arrival of number 67, eastbound. Thirty minutes later, a similar whistle told him that number 88, en route to Colorado, was pulling in.

Dao Chi waited and was dismayed to see Raymond Crocker appear at the door with more hot water. Time was running short. He knew he had to leave the Inn with Su Chang no later than 4:30 for his scheme to work.

The session continued until 4:10 when it looked like it was finally coming to an end. Edna thanked Su Chang for her hospitality and announced that she needed to leave. However, she agreed to another cup of tea and kept her seat.

Su Chang refilled all the cups.

Dao Chi's heart sunk. He had to strike. Now!

The unsuspecting hostess provided him with the perfect opportunity. She excused herself, walked into the bedroom and picked an assortment of carved ivory from her dresser to show her guests. In that instant, her back was toward him. He seized the opportunity and slid out from under the bed. Su Chang was horrified to see a face filling her mirror. Her scream suffocated in her throat as his hand clamped her mouth. She reacted violently, kicking her dresser, knocking off and smashing several bottles.

Steffi and Edna, astounded by the racket, shoved their cups aside and rushed in.

"Stop! Don't scream. I'll kill her!" Dao Chi ordered. The women stopped. A dagger was at Su Chang's throat. "All of you get down on the floor, face down, right now, hands behind your back!"

Stunned, they complied. Edna's fear quickly turned to hysteria and she began sobbing uncontrollably--having no idea of what was going to happen to them--or why. Steffi surprised herself by remaining remarkably composed. Su Chang was motionless.

Dao Chi set astride Su Chang's back, pinning her to the floor. He grabbed Edna who was trying to get to her feet, slammed her back on her belly and tied her hands behind her with the clothesline rope. As she begged for mercy, he bent her knees, yanked her ankles up and tied them to her wrists. Steffi saw that he was 'hog tying' her, a cruel way to immobilize the wretched woman.

Steffi considered making a break for it, a thought she quickly dismissed when she had a look at Edna's face. The color was draining away. She was turning deathly white. Steffi always thought Edna had a bad heart. Now she was sure of it. She decided that her best course of action would be to cooperate and offered no resistance when Dao Chi drug her over to him. Being calm was not her forte, but someone had to show some courage. She gritted her teeth, steeling herself against the pain and humillitation as the ropes dug into her flesh.

When he was finished, Dao Chi turned to Su Chang and asked, "Where are your silk scarves?" She motioned to her dresser. "Get up and get me two of them. Don't try to run away or I will kill these women." He let her up and switched the dagger to Edna's throat.

Su Chang handed him the scarves. "Get back down on your face!" he barked. He sat on her again and gagged Steffi and Edna with the scarves.

"You have a black dress and a hat with a veil in your closet. Put them on, now!" He said, letting Su Chang get up. Even though she was shaking so bad with fear that her knees would hardly support her, she stepped into the closet, exchanged her dress for the black one and emerged, pulling on the hat and veil. She finally got a good look at Dao Chi's face. A lump filled her throat. *The Tong! He's from the Tong!* She took three deep breaths to keep from fainting.

Steffi and Edna remained face down on the floor.

Dao Chi motioned to a valisc. "Pack three extra changes of clothes in that. Now! We are leaving on the train immediately."

Baffled, Su Chang complied.

Someone tapped on the front door. The dagger went back to her throat. "That's Raymond Crocker, our handyman. He's bringing more hot water," Su Chang explained.

51

"Tell him to come in. When he does, ask him to come back here as you want him to move your dresser. Do not arouse his suspicion."

Raymond heard her call, carried in another pot of scalding water, set it down, and walked into the bedroom.

He froze, not comprehending the scene before him. Two women hog-tied on the floor, the third one clothed in mourner's garb.

Dao Chi attacked from the rear. He grabbed the boy's mouth with one hand, locked him in a headlock with his free arm, and tried to kick his legs out from under him. But Raymond was wiry and tough. He'd been raised on the streets and knew how to fight. He ripped Dao Chi's hand from his mouth, wrenched free of the headlock, and saw his assailant's face. He couldn't believe it was the same cowboy that had flipped him a nickel earlier in the day. Dao Chi shoved him into a corner. Raymond fell back, kicked wildly, aiming for the groin, a futile effort as the tongsman was much too quick for such an amateurish move. He leveled Raymond with his own kick to the solar plexus, a stunning blow that knocked all the wind from the youth, tumbling him to the floor. Dao Chi pressed his advantage, forced the boy over, and tied and gagged him along with the others.

Dao Chi jerked his head up and fired a question, "Are there any people in the hallways or the foyer?" Raymond shook his head. Dao Chi knew that the hours from three to five are quiet times for hotels, making his chances of escape very good. Only the day clerk would be on duty at the hotel desk but Dao Chi thought they could slip by him. Even if he saw them, he wouldn't recognize Su Chang, now disguised as a woman in mourning, not an uncommon sight since Alexander had the only mortuary for miles around.

The train's whistle shattered his thoughts and goaded him to action. With his short dagger firmly against Su Chang's ribs, he picked up the valise in his free hand and said, "We are going to walk to the train station and take the train to St. Louis." A glance out the window told him there was no pedestrian traffic between the Inn and the depot.

He ushered Su Chang out, locked the door, and moved down to the foyer. The day clerk was engrossed in a newspaper. They slipped behind him and exited out onto the wooden sidewalk. In a few minutes they were at the depot where Dao Chi retrieved his cache of food. Seeing the ticket agent was nowhere around, he stepped over to the telegraph key and bent it slightly. Outside, they heard the conductor bellow, "All aboard, last call for Independence, Springfield, and St Louis!

Dao Chi and Su Chang hurried out and handed him their tickets.

"Going to St. Louis?" the conductor asked. Without waiting for an answer, he continued, "You'll have to change trains in Springfield. Is the lady in mourning?"

"Yes," Dao Chi answered.

"Well, there's passengers in cars one and two, but, if you want privacy go on to number three. It's empty and you can use it if you want. I won't be coming through to check tickets. You're the last people aboard. I've got the flu so I'm going back to the caboose and sleep until we get there."

His sour breath caused Dao Chi to take a step backward.

Dao Chi thanked him for the information and guided Su Chang through the first two cars. Most of the passengers acknowledged them with a smile or a nod. He noticed all blinds drawn on the south side of the train as the late afternoon sun was quite bright. *Good*, he thought, *no one will witness our departure.*

When they entered the empty car, he drew a blind aside. He could see Number 88 waiting on the south railway siding. Its baggage car was still open as the agent had returned to the depot for more freight. The casket had already been delivered by Harold Fry and loaded aboard.

Once again Su Chang was perplexed when Dao Chi explained, "We're getting off this train. We will get in the freight car of Number 88." He took her hand. They were

53

unobserved as they stepped down, crossed the tracks, and pulled themselves into the freight car.

Safely aboard, he pulled out the bottle of chloroform. Before Su Chang could react he soaked a handkerchief, lifted her veil, and smothered her face in the chemical. She was limp in a matter of seconds. The casket was at the far end of the car. Dao Chi, staggered by the weight of the unconscious body, lifted Su Chang up, placed her in the casket, then changed from his black cowboy hat and chaps into the plaid shirt, canvas pants, and campaign hat. He was no longer the Anglo cowboy. He was a Chinese coolie, escorting a casket for his employer.

The depot agent threw on a load of barbed wire for delivery to Trinidad, Colorado. He looked inside and saw Dao Chi sitting with the casket. He nodded a greeting to Dao Chi who nodded back. Then, with a mighty tug, he slammed and latched the heavy door.

Number 67 departed on time. Dao Chi could hear her laboring, her iron wheels spinning on the rails as she built up a full head of steam. He watched in quiet satisfaction as car after car passed by. He was pleased and smiled with glee. Car number 3 would arrive at Springfield with no one aboard.

A few minutes later, Number 88's whistle shrieked. The cars jerked and clanged as the huge machine came to life. Dao Chi braced himself and peered out. He saw several little boys running alongside, pelting the rail cars with hard cinders and gravel.

He knew that the next few hours would determine the success or failure of his mission. All was quiet in the casket. He guessed that his captive should awaken in about an hour. But he agonized. *What if I gave her too much chloroform?*

CHAPTER 10

MALCOLM, BEN, AND CHESTER

When Malcolm walked into the house on Friday evening, all was quiet. *That's right*, he remembered, *Steffi went to a meeting at Su Chang's and left the boys at Molly's place.* He looked around for some food. It was 4:30. He was already hungry. He went out to the well house, pulled a jar of milk out of the holding tank, then went to the smoke house. A smoked hog was cut up, packaged, and waiting. He located a pack of pork chops and went back to the house.

It was overcast and beginning to drizzle. Soon it would be dark. He knew that Steffi would stay overnight at Molly's house rather than try to drive home with the boys. Tonight, he would eat alone.

The cook stove had been banked since noon. He threw on some wood, shook the grates, opened the damper, and put the chops on.

He went back to the barn and lit a lantern and took another look at his calves.

He could tell if an animal was ailing by rubbing its nose to see if it was dry. As he suspected, several had dry noses. He would have to check them again in the morning. No one would buy sick steers. The fear of an epidemic was real. An entire herd--along with the rancher that owned them--could be wiped out in a matter of days. He knew that six hundred fever-ridden cattle were shot within the past year causing two ranches to hit the auction block within thirty days. The banks wound up with the land and the ranchers and their families moved away.

Back in the house, he rescued the blackening chops off the stove, shoved them onto his plate and sat down. He dug absent mindedly at them with his fork, then, pushed the plate aside and buried his head in his hands. He feared the worst. *Tomorrow will either make us or break us. First Andersonville, now this.*

Ben Wang was also setting down to supper, but he was in the Cattleman's Hotel Cafe in Medicine Lodge. He wouldn't get home tonight, either, because his trip hit a snag. He'd gone to pick up a large cook stove coming by wagon from Wichita. A telegram greeted him at the hotel. The shipment would be a day late. Ben cursed his luck but welcomed a night away from his business. Su Chang would understand and the delay would give him a chance do some reading. The hotel sold him a three-day-old copy of the Sunday Kansas City News for a nickel. He glanced over the first few pages.

Skirmishes with the Indians and U. S. Cavalry were still occurring along the Mexican border in Arizona and up in Montana. Bitter struggles were being waged among the giant railway companies who were competing for government franchises to lay thousands of miles of track. Gold and silver activity was strong in California and the western territories.

The Congressional page discussed the ways the government was spending, or planning to spend, the nation's wealth. A particular item caught his attention:

Congress appoints committee to study feasibility of laying another transatlantic telegraph cable from the east coast to London. Copper is the metal of choice to be used in the manufacture of the thousands of tons of wire that will be required. Since it is in short supply other metals are being tested.

Ben knew little about copper but he did know it would take a tremendous amount of it to provide enough cable to stretch across the Atlantic. He wondered how they would finance such a huge project. *Probably issue stocks and bonds*, he speculated, knowing that investment bankers on the east coast would put together the offering. He knew that no traditional banks could handle a deal of that magnitude.

The article was interesting but it didn't apply to him. He stuck the paper in his bag and started up to his room. A messenger boy stopped him. "Sir, here's a telegram for you." Ben took the envelope, handed the boy a dime and muttered, "Probably another delay on the stove."

He thumbed open the envelope. The message wasn't what he expected. It said, <u>Emergency-Stop-Come home-Stop-Urgent-Stop</u>. It was signed by Shorty.

"Do you want to send a reply?" the boy asked. "No. I must leave right now," Ben replied and threw the shocked lad a five dollar gold piece. "Here, pay my bill and keep the rest. It's for you. I have no time to waste."

Chester Zimmerman was at the bank as usual on Friday. But he wasn't reading the Sunday News. Several back issues were stacked up that he'd never opened. Pressing matters at the bank demanded most of his attention, and he was behind on his reading all the time. Among other things, the J. T. Smith note was due and J. T. wanted to skip the payment and have the note extended. Chester hated to do that. He'd gone overboard when he financed J. T. It took a fortune to stock a mercantile store because of the wide range of merchandise required. Chester knew that when he made the loan but the community was in need of a decent store. Nevertheless, he expected timely payments on the note. He felt a bit queasy when J. T. told him how much credit he'd extended to ranchers and farmers--money being repaid slowly due to the drought that withered their crops and livestock. To compound the problem, J. T. was on the bank board and the loan created a conflict of interest. Chester had to press for more collateral if the loan was to be re-written and J. T. wouldn't like that. The real question would be: "How can he come up with additional collateral at this time?"

Chester put on his hat and coat, blew out the lamps, and left by the private side entrance.

It was a brief walk home. He was a little irritated that Edna wasn't there to start supper. He knew she was over at Su Chang's promoting another one of her grand social schemes. There were plusses and minuses to her constant social ventures, but he knew all of it was important to his business so he tolerated it, even though it all seemed a bit frivolous to a man who dealt in hard cash every day.

He was hungry. He'd missed his dinner since two of the tellers were sick and he had to fill in at one of their windows, right at noon when several depositors came in.

He decided to walk over to the Goodnite Inn and have some coffee. When Edna's meeting was over, they could eat supper there.

Shorty was sweeping out his barbershop. He called out when Chester entered the foyer, "Howdy, Chester. You ain't seen our boy Raymond around town have you? He's plumb disappeared."

"No. "Course I been at the bank all day. Isn't he usually around here?"

"Yeah, but I haven't seen him for quite awhile. His job is to keep plenty of hot water on hand and he sweeps out when we close. Last time I saw him he was taking some water up to Su Chang. Must've been two hours or so ago."

"My wife is up there at a meeting. Her and Steffi. They've been there since about 3 O'clock. Have you seen any of them come down?"

"No, I been right here cuttin' hair all day. I'd of seen 'em."

"That's mighty strange. Is Ben in the restaurant?"

"No, he went to Medicine Lodge. Got a new stove comin' in. Since it's gettin' dark, he'll probably stay there overnight. That's what he usually does."

A frown creased Chester's brow. He didn't want to give the impression of the overly worried husband. After all Edna was over 21.

"When did you say was the last time Raymond took water upstairs?"

"Gosh, it's been two and a half or three hours. Somethin' like that."

Still not wanting to express his anxiety, Chester said, "Well, I think I'll go up and see if the party is about over. They can't last much longer without hot water." He smiled weakly.

"Wait a minute and I'll walk up with you. If Raymond is up there loafing, that boy and I are going to have a talk!" Shorty replied.

Upstairs, Chester knocked repeatedly. There was no reply. Shorty's foot crunched a piece of paper. He picked it up and observed, "Somebody tried to stick a note under the door."

It was the telegram, the one Smooth Mouth Sam had sent to J. T. Smith. Moses Farmer had left it there earlier when his knock on the door went unanswered.

They read it together. "I don't know what this means but I don't like it!" Chester's, voice reflected his agitation. "Go down and get a pass key from the night clerk. We're going in!"

Shorty was back in seconds and handed the key to Chester.

They entered, saw nothing out of order, and were startled to hear a bumping noise coming from the bedroom.

Chester stepped into the bedroom. At the sight of the three gagged and hog-tied victims, he recoiled back, banging into Shorty. He jerked a derringer from his jacket pocket. Shorty was carrying a straight edge razor. Seeing they weren't in danger, they dropped to their knees, cut the women's bonds, then freed Raymond who had been banging his head on the dresser to alert them.

As Shorty ministered to Steffi and Raymond, rubbing circulation back into their near paralyzed limbs while they blurted out their incredible story, Chester pulled Edna into his arms and stared at her, unwilling to accept what had happened. She had not survived the ordeal. Her heart, never strong, had stopped. The society queen of Alexander had attended her last tea. Chester never looked up. He stared straight into her unseeing eyes as he rocked her back and forth, frozen with grief. Then, as though the dam had broken, his body began to heave as he began sobbing. They were gasping, choking sobs that unnerved everyone. Steffi moved quickly to his side in an effort to console him.

Shorty, casting his eyes to the floor, very uncomfortable at witnessing the town banker in a near state of complete breakdown, said, "I'll tell Herman to get ahold of the night Marshal. I'll be right back!" He took the stairs three at a time down to the clerk's desk, told him what had happened, instructed him to locate the Marshal, and rushed back upstairs.

Steffi and Raymond, still stunned, sat quietly trying to console Chester while they awaited the arrival of 'the law'.

Herman found Nate Christopher, the acting marshal, playing dominoes in the saloon next door. He blurted out the story of the apparent murder of Edna, the abduction of Su Chang, and the hog-tying of Steffi and Raymond, a story that was met with near disbelief by everyone in the saloon.

Nate abandoned his game and charged up to the apartment. After a brief questioning of all parties, he said, "Shorty, go over and roust out the depot man. He's got to wire the sheriff at Medicine Lodge and get him over here. This ain't no job for me. Man, I don't know nothin' about handling a situation like this!"

Shorty headed for the door. "Wait a minute!" Nate ordered. "Stop downstairs. Get one of the boys to ride out to Malcolm's place to tell him what's goin' on."

It was almost forty-five minutes before Shorty reported back, "Sorry it took so long. I found the agent O. K. but he couldn't get the telegraph to work right. Took all this time to find out someone had bent the key just a little and that threw it off. Dadgumdest thing you ever heard of! Anyway, he finally got it fixed and the sheriff got our message and wired back. He said everyone is to stay in this room until he gets here. And to call Harold Fry, since he's the acting coroner, to take a look at Edna."

It took two hours of hard riding for Sheriff Rolf Hanson to get to Alexander, a punishing ride that left his horse lathered. He pulled up at the saloon and asked if someone would take his horse over to Binford's Livery Stable. It was worth two bits and he got a quick volunteer. He ignored a barrage of questions, told everyone to keep calm, and headed for the inn. Shorty showed up and made a path through the crowd. "Follow me," he said. "I'll take you up."

Malcolm hit the landing just then and ran upstairs behind them.

Rolf whirled around, his hand over his holster, and demanded, "Where do you think you're goin', cowboy?"

Shorty intervened. "It's OK. He's the husband of one of the women upstairs. Malcolm Frazier."

"Sorry," Rolf said. "Didn't know who you were."

They shook hands and Shorty ushered them in.

Rolf was no slouch when it came to crime investigation. He'd had training at the State Marshal's headquarters in Topeka and earned a temporary U. S. Marshal's badge in addition to his Sheriff's badge.

If he'd known Ben was in Medicine Lodge, he would have accompanied him back to Alexander. But, he didn't, so Ben came back alone with no idea of what had happened at the Inn and irritated with the disruption of his plans.

Ernest C. Frazier

CHAPTER 11

THE INVESTIGATION

The townsfolk, waiting for some official news about the kidnapping, milled around downstairs, spreading rumors like wildfire.

Upstairs, Rolf could see that Steffi and Harold Fry were the only two coherent enough to make sense. Raymond was too excited and Chester was in shock.

After brief introductions, Harold confirmed the fact that they had a corpse on their hands. Rolf asked him to remain in the room with Edna's body and console Chester. Steffi was holding onto Malcolm and began telling him what had happened. Rolf interrupted and asked her to tell the story from start to finish, filling in all the details that she could remember.

She had barely opened her mouth when Ben, who had ridden in and worked his way through the crowd, burst in and asked what had happened.

Rolf explained, "Ben, Su Chang has been kidnapped and Edna has been killed. I just got here myself. Steffi and Raymond were tied up on the floor and Steffi is starting to tell us what happened. I know this is tough for you, but we've all go to sit and listen while she talks."

Ben was exhausted but his fatigue vanished at the news of Su Chang's abduction and the sight of Edna lying dead on his bedroom floor. Stunned, he sat down with the others, his mind swimming with unanswered questions.

Steffi told them of the meeting with the three ladies and the sudden appearance and attack by the mysterious cowboy.

Raymond interrupted, "That's the same hombre that asked me about Ben and Su Chang earlier today. He wanted to know where they lived and flipped me a nickel. Later, he knocked me down when I came in here with the water!"

Rolf made a note of that, then nodded at Steffi to continue.

"It was obvious that Su Chang had no idea who the man was or why he wanted to take her away. He gave us no opportunity to reason with him, just started tying us up, really tight, and gagged us with these scarves. Then he told Su Chang to change into a black dress and made her put on a black hat with a veil."

"She was never tied up?" the sheriff asked.

Steffi shook her head, "No, he had to leave her free to walk downstairs. Nobody could tell who she was in that veil and mourning dress."

"Do you have any idea where they went?"

"He told her to pack a bag with three changes of clothes before they left. Then he told her they were going to take a train ride."

"I need to know your opinion about Edna's death. Do you have any idea if he did anything that caused her to die, such as striking or choking her?"

"No," Steffi quietly replied, her voice cracking with nervous fatigue. "He didn't hit her, but he tied us all very tightly. Edna wears a full corset. We all know her heart wasn't strong. It was difficult enough to breathe since we were trussed up like hogs. I don't think she could breathe properly with that corset on. Then, just the strain of the whole ordeal probably was too much for her heart to handle."

Steffi began to sob as she completed her statement. Rolf glanced at Malcolm's eyes. They told him that Steffi was at the end of her emotional rope so he switched to Raymond.

"Raymond, run over to the depot. See if you can find the agent and get him over here. Tell him to bring his passenger records for all trains that left today. You come back with him. I may need you around here."

The boy was out the door in a flash, eager to burn off some nervous energy, bursting with pride at being called on the help in the investigation. He was at the station in a matter of minutes and beat on the door until Cletus, who was upstairs in his quarters, came down to see what was going on.

"I knew somethin' was haywire when they had me send a wire to Ben about an emergency, but I sure didn't expect no murder," Cletus said as he gathered up the information for the sheriff.

In a few moments they slipped through the back entrance of the hotel to avoid the crowd.

Rolf opened his questioning of the depot agent, verifying that tickets had been purchased for two adults by a strange cowboy dressed in black hat and chaps. They were booked on number 67 to St. Louis.

"What did the woman look like?"

"I don't know. The cowboy bought the tickets in advance. They probably got on the train later while I was loadin' freight."

"What kind of freight?"

"No freight on number 67. I was loading some stuff on number 88. It was on the siding gettin' ready to go west."

Rolf repeated his question.

"Barbed wire to Trinidad," Cletus answered. "Also, somethin' real strange was goin' on. A body was embalmed here this week. The same cowboy that was goin' to St. Louis asked me to ship the casket to Trinidad and on to Durango. He sent a helper, looked like he might have been Chinese, to escort the body."

"Wait a minute!" Harold Fry rose to make some corrections. "There wasn't no body embalmed here this week. That cowboy came to my place and bought an empty casket to be shipped home to bury his mother in. When you and me loaded that casket on the train there wasn't nobody in it!"

Cletus pondered Harold's comments for a minute, then replied, "Well, he said there was a body in the coffin. That's what he told me, and I know another man was aboard with the coffin when the train headed west. He was sittin' by it when I slid the door shut. Nobody would have any reason to ride all that way in a freight car with an empty coffin."

Rolf was scribbling notes like mad. All this was getting out of hand and didn't make any sense. Also, he had Edna's body to deal with but he wasn't ready to release her to the mortuary just yet.

"OK, Cletus, can you wire Springfield? See if you can get ahold of the conductor as soon as the train stops. Ask him if Su Chang and the cowboy actually got on the train here. If they're aboard, he's to call the law to take 'em off. If they aren't aboard, I want to know if any of the passengers saw them on the train. Make sure they verify the descriptions. Tell 'em what kind of clothes they were wearing."

"The train pulls into to Springfield in nine minutes," Cletus pulled his massive watch out of his overalls. "She's always on time so I'll get a wire goin' right now. She only lays over there for seventeen minutes. What kind of clothes were they wearin' when they left the hotel? I never saw 'em at the station."

After obtaining a quick description, Cletus left down the back stairway and raced back to begin transmitting.

"Come back as soon as you have an answer!" Rolf yelled after him. "We may have to wire Durango and check out that weird empty casket story before the night is over."

"Ben, I'm going to ask you some questions, but, first, we have to deal with this situation." Rolf turned his attention to Chester and Harold.

"Harold, you can take Edna out now. Chester, you can go with him if you want to, or you can stay here while I talk with Ben."

"I think I'll stay. She'll be in good hands and I don't want to miss anything that's being said." Chester had regained his composure and wanted to get as much information as he could.

The mortician walked downstairs to get some help. In a few minutes he reappeared with two volunteers. The removed the closet door from its hinges. Using it as a stretcher, they carried Edna out the front door and walked into a blizzard of questions from the crowd. They told the people they'd have to wait for a statement by the sheriff, pushed through and went on to the mortuary.

Upstairs, Rolf turned his attention to Ben.

"Ben, do you have any idea why anyone would kidnap Su Chang and commit these other crimes."

"Sheriff Hanson, you should know that we came to Alexander to find a safe haven. Are you familiar with secret Chinese societies known as tongs?"

The sheriff replied that he had never heard of such a thing

"Wait a minute," Chester interjected, "here's a telegram for J. T. Smith from a prospector named Smooth Mouth Sam. Look, it mentioned that Ben should beware of The Tong. I forgot about it until just now."

Ben and Rolf read the telegram together.

Ben explained, "The tongs were formed by Chinese businessmen, sort of a trading alliance among themselves, and they offered many benefits to their members. Over the years some were taken over by Chinese gangsters. They demand protection money from their own people, took over the opium trade, prostitution, and loan sharking. They operate on the west coast and are moving inland. They cornered me on the ship that was taking us to San Francisco. I refused their demands for extortion as I was unaware of their viciousness. They attacked me. I had a pistol and shot one of them in the stomach. I'm sure it killed him. I found out he was a nephew of Kai Mang who is chief of the Tong of The Black Hand in San Francisco. Since I had a gun they let me leave their cabin, but warned me that my family would never escape their wrath. The next morning, my mother, who was on the ship with us, was found floating in the water. They had broken her neck and thrown her overboard in the night. My uncle, the warlord, Ke Li, was on the ship. He knows of The Tong and said they would track us down, kill me, and either sell Su Chang to white slavers or keep her for Kai Mang. We escaped and made our way to Durango, Colorado. That's where we met Smooth Mouth Sam. He was being treated by a doctor there. He thought that Kansas would be a good place for us to settle. But, we never mentioned the tong to him. I have no idea how he found out about them."

"Good Lord," said Rolf, "I thought I'd heard it all, but, that's the dadgumdest thing I ever heard of! It sounds like the tong trailed you down here. Is that the way you figure it?"

"There is no doubt. They have my wife. We must act fast! I will pay for men or anything else it takes to get her back!"

"OK, Ben, we'll do everything we can," the sheriff assured him. "Right know, I think we'd better get J. T. up here and see what he knows about Smooth Mouth Sam."

"Raymond, go downstairs and see if J. T. is there. If not, run over to his store and bring him back. Here's a quarter. Stop and get a pot of hot coffee and some cups. We may be here for awhile." Seeing the look of expectancy on the boy's face, he flipped him another quarter and said, "I guess you don't drink coffee. Here's a quarter for you. Get yourself a hamburger or a piece of pie. You're looking a little scrawny, but make sure you find J. T. before you stop!"

Cletus came back in and reported, "I wired Martin Phelps in Springfield, the conductor. He says they got on the train here. Says the lady was in mourning and they got into car number three which was empty. Several passengers saw 'em go in there. Now here's the rub. Only three passengers, people in the first car, got off at Springfield. Nobody saw anyone else get off. Martin searched the whole train and they ain't on board. He says there's no way they could've got off without bein' seen. I can tell you they didn't jump off along the way. The grade and trestles and bridges are too high. You'd break your legs. They just vanished into thin air!"

"No, it doesn't make a lick of sense," Rolf scratched his head, then, continued. "Are you sure they searched the train from one end to the other?"

"Car number three was the last car before the caboose. They didn't climb in the caboose. The brakeman would've seen 'em. They didn't go back into the other cars 'cause the passengers would have seen them, and, like I said, they weren't about to jump off and kill themselves!"

Someone knocked on the door. Malcolm walked over and let J. T. Smith in.

"J. T., I guess you know what's happened here by now?" Rolf asked.

"I hear what everyone else hears, but I don't know exactly what happened. Lots of rumors floatin' around town," J. T. answered. He put his hand on Chester's shoulder. "Sure sorry about Edna. I know it's got to be a terrible shock."

"Appreciate it, J. T. Everyone's bein' good about it."

J. T.turned to Ben and said, "Don't worry Ben. We've got the best sheriff in the state on this case. There's a whole posse forming downstairs if Rolf needs 'em."

Ben nodded silently, mired deep in his own thoughts.

"J. T., what do you know about the old miner that sent you this telegram?" Rolf began his questioning. "It was found under the doorway here."

"I've grubstaked him a few times when I operated out of St. Joe. He always paid off in the past. He's out in Arizona lookin' for a big strike but isn't havin' a lot of luck. He's fallin' behind on what he owes me. I'm holding his mine stock for collateral. That's why he keeps me informed. He's gettin' way behind."

"How would he know about the tong looking for Ben?"

Raymond walked in with the coffee, poured everyone a cupful, and started munching on an onion laden hamburger.

"I don't know," J. T. replied. "One thing did happen though that might give us some ideas."

"Ben," he asked, "what's the name of the tong that's after you?"

"The Tong of The Black Hand," replied Ben.

"That's it!" cried J. T. "When Peg Leg Charlie was in getting grubstaked a couple of months ago--he's an old prospecting buddy of Smooth Mouths'--he told me he'd heard from a cowboy that Smooth Mouth had got branded by a couple of Chinamen." Then, with a glance at Ben, changed his language to a more respectful tone and continued; "Chinese men way out at Holbrook, Arizona. The cowboy didn't know anything about it except that the brand was shaped like a hand. Peg Leg said he was going to look up Smooth Mouth down in Arizona and find out the whole story."

"Hmm," Rolf muttered, then looked back at Ben. "It sounds like the tong knew that you'd met Smooth Mouth Sam in Durango. But, why in the world would they follow him all the way to Holbrook? They must have wanted information about you and Su Chang but Smooth Mouth wasn't talking so they decided to torture him."

"Go back to the depot and wire the Sheriff in Holbrook. I want to know everything he can find out about that incident," Rolf barked his instructions, then softened his voice as he remembered the depot agent wasn't his employee. "Anyway, let me know as soon as you have an answer. I'll really appreciate it. Also, do something else. Wire the Sheriff in Durango and tell him to search the freight car for the casket and the escort. I want him to hold that man for questioning. Tell the Sheriff this is in connection with a murder and kidnapping case so he'll know we mean business."

Within minutes Cletus completed his transmission to Holbrook and was awaiting a reply. When he started tapping out his message to Durango, he realized the wire was dead. He knew that either a storm had snapped the line or someone had cut it. Since the weather had been fair for several days, he could only suspect the worst. He wired the railway's Kansas City office to advise them of the downed line, knowing it could take several days to locate the break. In an attempt to expedite matters he requested that Kansas City wire his message direct to Denver who could relay it to Durango. In a few minutes Kansas City responded with a message saying that Denver was also having trouble on their line to Durango but they would keep trying.

Cletus scratched his head and cursed the inefficiency of the railroad, wondering why he hadn't become a muleskinner instead of a depot agent. The clattering of his telegraph key brought him back to reality. The answer to his wire to Holbrook was coming in. He recorded the message, tore it off his pad and rushed back to the inn to report to Rolf.

Rolf read it and said, "It looks like Smooth Mouth Sam did have a run in with two Chinamen. Three cowboys rode up just as they was branding Smooth Mouth and shot one of them dead. The other one escaped and the sheriff thinks he headed for California but they never could pick up his trail. Smooth Mouth told him they were pumping him for information about the whereabouts of Ben and Su Chang. Said they had unfinished business from China with them."

"What about your wire to Durango?"

Cletus explained the problems and the probability of a cut telegraph wire.

"You know," Rolf spoke as his mind and intuition began to work in tandem, "I think we need to notify the various sheriff's departments all the way to St. Louis to keep searching. It's possible they got off somewhere between here and there. Possible but not probable. I think a switch occurred before they left here and Su Chang may be on her way to Durango instead of St. Louis. She could be in that casket with the kidnapper riding along. I got a hunch the whole idea of them going to St. Louis was just a scheme to throw us off. I've got a strong feeling in my belly about that. But, we need to be safe. Cletus, send an open wire to all sheriffs from here to St. Louis. Advise them to be on the lookout, just in case they did go east."

Cletus left and Nate Christopher came in to see how things were progressing.

"Nate, I think I'm going to have to go to Durango. I suspect that Su Chang's captor pulled a switch on us and they are headed there, not to St. Louis as we first suspected. Also, we can't get a telegram to Durango 'cause the line is down. That means I've got to go since everything Ben tells me indicates Su Chang's life is in danger. I carry a temporary U. S. Marshal's badge which, is good for one year until I complete my training. That gives me authority to enter other states as a lawman and I can deputize others, as I need 'em. Nate, I need two of the best men from this area to go with me. When we get to Colorado, I can get additional help from the Sheriff there. Who do you recommend?"

Before Nate could answer, Malcolm stepped forward, "Sheriff, I want to be one of those men. I can ride and shoot and I'd sure like to have a crack at the people responsible for all of this. Not only did they kill Edna and kidnap Su Chang, they could have just as easily killed Steffi and Raymond. I want to be on that train with you tonight!"

"Sheriff, I want to go too," Ben volunteered as he rose to stand next to Malcolm.

"Ben," I don't know if that is too smart an idea. I understand your feelings but remember: the tong may be after you as well as Su Chang. I'd rather have others involved in this, not you since you are a target. Your life might not be worth a plugged nickel once we get to Durango. I think you'd better stay here. We'll keep you posted, and we want you here safely when we bring Su Chang back."

Ben let Rolf's words sink in before he slowly sat down, nodding his head and saying, "You are probably right. I'll stay behind, but I don't want to."

Rolf put his hand on his shoulder, "Ben, that is the right decision. You would make a fine deputy, but this just isn't the right situation for that right now."

Then he said, "Malcolm, think hard about this. You've got a wife and a family. Are you sure you want to go? Chances are we are going to get involved with the Chinese tong and there could be gunplay. Sounds like they play mighty rough so you really want to be certain that this is the trip for you. I hate to say it but some of us may not make it back."

"Rolf, I've already thought about it. There just isn't anything to discuss. Count me in," Malcolm answered with conviction.

"Ok, you're in. We need one more. Who do you boys recommend?" Rolf addressed Malcolm and Nate.

"I vote for Angus McDougal if he wants to come," replied Malcolm. "What do you think, Nate?"

"Angus is stronger than a bull and lightning fast," Nate replied. "If I was going, I'd want him along."

"Raymond," Rolf spoke to the boy again, "go down and see if Angus is in the crowd. If he is, ask him to come up here with you. Don't tell him or anyone else what we are talking about."

Raymond left and returned momentarily with Angus who extended his bear-like hand to the Sheriff: "Howdy, I'm McDougal. Raymond here says you want to talk to me."

Rolf, a large man in his own right felt dwarfed by the huge Scotsman. His hand was totally engulfed by McDougal's and he could see why the others wanted him along.

The giant Scot eagerly agreed to the sheriff's request. He had a part time helper who could keep his shop open, and, since he was single, family was not a consideration.

Rolf, Malcolm, and Angus completed their travel plans and arranged to meet at the depot fifteen minutes before the westbound train departed for Durango. Rolf deputized them on the spot and they parted to pack weapons, clothing, and food for the trip. They went down the back stairway, not wanting to be confronted by the crowd below.

Steffi fought back tears all the way to Molly's house where she would pick up the boys. She knew what Malcolm was doing was right, but she also remembered the look in Dao Chi's eyes as he trussed her and the others up with his rope. She knew Malcolm would be facing a trained killer!

Ernest C. Frazier

CHAPTER 12

CAPTOR AND CAPTIVE

Su Chang, her head throbbing, awakened to the staccato click, click, click, of wheels racing through the night on twin ribbons of steel. She tried to sit up but had no room to move. Her memory flashed back to when Dao Chi administered the chloroform and she remembered the casket. While fearing what she might find, she nevertheless gathered her strength and forced open the lid. The light in the freight seemed brilliant. When her vision cleared, she saw Dao Chi.

Neither spoke and she studied his face. His features told her that he was from one of the southern provinces of China. If that were correct, she surmised, he probably was from the peasant class, hired to do the dirty work of the Tong and was unaccustomed to addressing a lady such as herself.

She boldly asked, "Who are you and what do you want with me?"

Dao Chi looked at the floor and seemed confused by her abruptness. As suspected, his answer came in a southern dialect.

"You are a captive of the Tong of the Black Hand. I am taking you to Colorado at the order of Kai Mang, my master."

"Your tong has killed my mother-in-law and now you are kidnapping me all because my husband refused to pay tribute. You are a fool. We are no longer in China. Life in America is valuable. If you deliver me to them, my blood will be on your hands regardless of whether they kill me or hold me captive. You are nothing but a peasant hired to do their dirty work."

Her voice strengthened, "Do you know that you will be hanged or imprisoned for life if I am killed or taken as a slave? Tell me; is your life worth nothing? Are you foolish enough to believe that you can get away will this stupid action? Are you a complete fool?" Su Chang pressed her taunting questions and remarks as a flicker of distress creased his brow. Feeling more confident, she stepped out of the casket and walked over to where he was sitting.

"I am thirsty," she continued as her mouth was bone dry. "Are those jugs of water for drinking?"

"You may drink from one of them. The other is for washing. I also have a bag of food for us as it is a long ride to Durango," Dao Chi pointed to the provisions.

"Durango!" she jeered. "Do you actually think we'll ever get to Durango? Don't you know that telegraph messages will advise all lawmen of my abduction? This train will be stopped long before we get that far. It would take almost two days to get there."

"You say I am stupid," Dao Chi whined, intimidated by his beautiful captive who displayed no fear. She was the type of woman he could only dream of, well educated-she addressed him in his dialect-and, very wealthy as her clothing was of the finest silk. "But, do not underestimate me," he warned, trying to strengthen his position and re-establish his authority over Su Chang. "You must understand, we will get to Durango. The telegraph wires have been cut. The Tong has taken every precaution to see that we arrive safely."

Su Chang sat down on a barrel and steadied herself against the constant swaying of the car. She was nauseated by the chloroform and upset by Dao Chi's comments.

She decided to take a softer approach in her conversation and attempt to appeal to Dao Chi's senses of reason and, hopefully, fair play.

"Why are you involved with the Tong? What gain or reward can you expect that will pay you for the extreme risk and danger to your life? You seem like an intelligent man. What drives you to do this?"

Dao Chi's jaw tensed as these piercing questions were put to him. Of course he knew she was drawing him out, making him think and hopefully respond to questions that he didn't have to answer. He knew he should ignore her but he felt compelled to explain his actions.

"When I was a young boy, famine spread throughout our province and many people starved to death. It was common practice for a family to kill their infant daughters to avoid the expense of feeding them or sell them to a wealthy buyer. I have a sister. Our father sold her to the Tong. She is now living in the household of Kai Mang in San Francisco. That is probably where you will be taken. I am compelled to obey the orders from Kai Mang. Failure to do so would result in my death and my sister would also die. You now understand that nothing will stop me from delivering you as ordered." His eyes hardened again as he spoke, his resolve strengthened with the reminder of the penalties for failure.

Su Chang, disheartened by his revelation, at least understood his motivation. Unfortunately, it appeared he had no choice but to deliver her as planned.

"The train will stop in Trinidad around midnight and unload their freight. You'll have to be back in the casket since they'll come into this car." Dao Chi spoke again with authority.

"If I promise to be quiet will you not use the chloroform on me again?" Su Chang pleaded.

"I'll make that decision when we get to Trinidad. Try to get some sleep now. The floor is rough but there is a blanket. I'll wake you up later."

Su Chang couldn't get comfortable. She finally dozed off only to be jarred awake by squealing brakes.

"It is time to get back into the casket?" Dao Chi shook her shoulder.

"I need to use the toilet. Is there none here?"

"Go to the back of the car. There are two empty buckets. Use one of them."

Su Chang did as instructed, returned, and laid down in the casket. She had determined that further discussion with Dao Chi was futile. The last thing she remembered was the wet handkerchief covering her face. Fearful that she may never waken, she began to pray.

CHAPTER 13

TRANSFERRING STOCK

The monthly meeting of the bank board was delayed a full thirty minutes because everyone was talking about the murder and kidnapping. Chester was planning Edna's funeral and the last thing he wanted to do was conduct a director's meeting, but he had no other choice as the vice-chairman, George Norton, was inexperienced in such matters. Also, the touchy question of the loan to J. T. Smith, now very much in arrears, needed immediate attention. Chester knew that only he could chair a meeting addressing that sensitive issue.

Ben was present even though only a day had passed since Su Chang's abduction. He related what he knew of the incident and of his problems with the tong.

When J. T. Smith came in, running late due to problems at his store, a pall settled over the room. Chester hastily called the meeting to order.

Traditional business items were addressed and disposed of in rubber-stamp fashion. Then the matter of delinquent loans came under discussion. J. T. sat quietly as the list was read. The $25,000 he owed was by far the largest over-due loan in the portfolio. No interest had been paid since their last meeting even though J. T. had assured them that it would be.

"Boys," J. T. began when given the opportunity to speak, "you know how rough business has been with the drought and all. Nobody is paying on time. But, as a director, I understand the position I've got us all in. I know you need payment now or it'll take more collateral to keep me in the game. Most of you know that I've already pledged about everything I own. I could liquidate the business and maybe come out with enough to pay off the loan, but, that would mean no more store in town. The

79

only thing I have of value except for the inventory and my bank stock, is the mining stock that Smooth Mouth Sam assigned to me. I don't know what value it has now but it might be worth a lot some day. They are hitting a little copper out there but the market is slow. If you call the note now, I'll have to sell out. If you'll take the mining stock and release me from the debt, I can stay in business. I know it sounds like a tough proposition and I'm truly sorry it's come to this, but my back is up against the wall."

J. T.'s voice cracked as he outlined his sad financial condition. Everyone squirmed in their seat. They knew he was having some difficulty, but assumed his problems could be worked out. Instinctively they turned to Chester. The bank president would have to guide them in their decision.

Chester opened up: "Well, we've got a real problem here. If J. T. liquidates, the town loses the best mercantile store for miles around. If we take the mining stock and it proves to be worthless, the bank loses $25,000. We need to have a private discussion regarding this, J. T., so I think you should set out in the lobby until we call you back in."

J. T. agreed and went out. Nobody expressed any interest in the mining stock except Ben. He was the only one aware of the government's interest in copper and he agreed that the mining stock could have growth potential. The others were much more concerned with the mercantile store. It would practically ruin their fledgling town if it went out of business. They decided to take his bank stock and mining stock in full payment of the debt and let J. T. stay in business. But, he would have to resign from the board.

J. T. was asked back in and advised of the board's decision. He thanked them for their consideration, signed over both stocks, and submitted his resignation.

"I'll advise Smooth Mouth to come to the bank to get his mining stock back," J. T. said. "I reckon it doesn't matter who he owes the money to. He'll just have to pay the bank instead of me."

The directors shook his hand and J. T. left the bank. It had been a sticky situation and they were glad it was over. Their main concern now was how to get their money out of Smooth Mouth Sam. The bank didn't want to get into the mining business. They wanted cash. Of course, none of them knew that many of their decisions were being made for them that very instant some 800 miles away on the Arizona-Mexico border.

Ernest C. Frazier

CHAPTER 14

TREACHERY IN TUCSON

When provisions ran low at the mine, Smooth Mouth and Hitch sent Levi on the five-day trip to Tucson. There were smaller towns around, Tombstone, Bisbee, and Willcox, but the assay office in Tucson would weigh their gold dust and analyze their copper ore in private. That made the long trip worthwhile. They knew of too many cases where claim jumpers ran off or killed mine operators when word of an important strike spread around. A trip to Tucson was a luxury that only occurred about once a year. When Levi's turn came up, he was ready to go.

The trail was dry and rutted but the old buckboard was up to it. Since their food supply was exhausted, Levi had to live on hard tack, beans, and salt pork. He was sick and tired of the monotonous fare and could hardly wait until he could sink his teeth into fresh meat. When he got to town, he tied up at The Cattleman's Roost, which advertised rooms, barbershop, and cafe. Inside they told him there was a livery stable out back. He could leave his horse and buckboard there for fifty cents a day. He signed up for room and board at two dollars a day. For another dollar he could get a bath, shave, haircut, and get his clothes washed. There were cheaper places in town but Levi was too tired to look around and the assay office was just a block away.

Levi spent an hour in the barber shop. He walked out feeling like a new man and went to the dining room for supper. He scanned the room. It was full of cattlemen, miners, and teamsters. He noticed that a card shark and a couple of other characters didn't bother to check their guns when they came but nobody said anything about it.

There was no shortage of conversation, but Levi decided to

83

listen instead of talk. He was quiet by nature and years of working as a prospector and miner hadn't done much to loosen his tongue. He was seated with the card shark who invited him to a game in his room that night, and a cattleman who had evidently spent too much time in the bar. As his tongue loosened, he displayed a roll of money, boasting that he'd sold several pens of calves at a good profit that afternoon. The card shark's attention went from Levi to the cattleman. Seated across the table were the two who hadn't checked their guns. They said very little but took in everything. Levi didn't like their looks. Their eyes showed no humor even when they smiled. *Probably deserters or hired gunslingers.* He finished his dinner and headed upstairs, wanting to be alone. The less anyone knew of his affairs the happier he would be.

The assay office opened at 9:00 AM and he was one of the first ones in. He asked an agent if they could meet in a private office. "Sure," the agent replied, "just have a seat. I'll be with you shortly. Here's the newspaper if you want to read it."

"Well, I'll look at the pictures," Levi laughed self-consciously. "I never did go to school so I ain't much on readin'."

"Too bad. Never know when you might learn something."

Levi opened the paper. There weren't any pictures so he put it down.

If he could read he would have found the front-page news most interesting. It predicted that the price of copper would skyrocket due to the construction of the transatlantic cable.

Within a few minutes, the agent ushered him into a private office and asked what he could do for him. Levi emptied the small pouch of gold dust they had gleaned over the past four months and said he wanted to sell it. It only took a moment for the agent to weigh it and offer four hundred and fifty dollars. Levi kept up on the gold market and knew that was a fair price.

"What else you got? You can't make a living minin' little dabs of gold like this, that's for sure," the agent asked, his eyes on Levi's gunnysack.

Levi dumped the sack onto the table. "Copper," he said, "but we didn't have no way to see how pure it is. We don't know nothin' about copper."

"It's copper ore alright, and I can run some tests on it," the agent offered. "Come back tomorrow and I'll give you an opinion. Are you finding quite a bit of it?" he asked. It was a seemingly innocent question.

"We ain't finding nothin' else. It's pretty discouraging when what you really want is gold. I'd guess we could haul out a wagonload every hour if we had a market for it. I'll be obliged if you can have it tested in the morning. I need to get on the road early."

"I have it ready by about eight o'clock."

"Good. I'll be in then. By the way, what is your name?"

"They just call me Jed."

"OK, see you tomorrow."

Levi's next stop was the General Store. He spent about one third of his proceeds on clothing, food, and miscellaneous items they needed at the mine. He spent the rest of the day wandering around town, eventually settling down at the hotel bar where he watched a high stakes poker game for an hour or so.

He answered the first bell for supper and was seated with the same people as before. This time, the cattleman was sober and was not in a talkative mood. The card shark was sullen as he'd lost heavily the night before, but now the two hard eyed gents across the table had softened up a bit and were a bit more friendly. Levi was cordial, but offered little information about himself. In fact, he became increasingly uncomfortable when they asked some rather pointed questions about his occupation, where he was from, and other items of information he considered personal. His answers were vague and he left the table as soon as he finished eating.

That night he slept fitfully and was glad when the sun came up. He was doubly pleased to see that the two hard eyed strangers were not at breakfast. He talked a little with the cattleman who was also leaving soon to return to his ranch up north along the Mogollon Rim. His name was Jacob Slattery and Levi hoped he'd run into him again someday.

Meanwhile, at the assay office, Jed was interrupted by a knock at the back door.

"Who's there?"

"Me and Bob," was the reply.

The assay agent opened up, quickly ushered the two in and re-bolted the door. If Levi had been there he would have recognized them as the two gunmen from the Cattlemen's Roost that he wanted to avoid.

"Howdy Sy, Bob." Jed offered his hand to both of them. "We ain't got a lot of time. We open in half an hour and some of the other clerks come in early."

"Well, what have you got?" Sy asked.

"Copper, tons of it, unlimited quantities, and the sap suckers mining it don't know what they got. I don't think they can read so they don't know what the government is fixin' to do." Jed practically rubbed his hands with glee as he related the information.

"Sounds almost too good to be true," replied Sy. "What if they talked to someone else who told them that the price is going to start jumpin'?"

"Ain't no way. This one miner come in here yesterday and wanted to meet in my private office. I guess him and his brother and their dad operate the mine. I don't think they trust nobody and don't waste much time talkin'." Jed was adamant in his reply. "Anyway, he is goin' to be in here first thing to see our assay report. It's highgrade copper, just what the government is lookin' for. In fact, it's as good or better than any we've ever seen around here. Here's my thinkin': I'll tell him it looks like pretty good stuff and I'll show him the current market quote." He grinned slyly and continued, "from last weeks paper. It was at an all time low then so he won't get excited. Anyway, gold miners can't see the value in other minerals and he ain't no different than the rest. He'll be disappointed but he'll go back to the mine with his supplies. If you boys want in this deal, just wait across the street on the loafer's bench. When he leaves the office, I'll walk out and kind of give him a salute goodbye. That way you'll know he's our man."

Sy asked, "I suppose you want your regular deal?"

"You bet. Five hundred now and five hundred when you bring in your first assay from the mine. I'm not a greedy man. You can keep the profits. Also, I don't want to hear nothin' about what have to do to the miners to get the mine. That is your business, not mine. All I do is sell information."

"Done. Give the man his gold," Sy ordered. "We'll be across the street. Don't keep us waitin'."

Bob handed over a pouch full of gold dust. Jed weighed out his share then and hurried them out the door.

Thirty minutes later the assay office opened for business and several customers walked in. A few minutes later Jed walked out with Levi, stopped, shook his hand, then offered a salute as they parted.

Sy and Bob recognized Levi from their stay at the Cattlemen's Roost.

Ernest C. Frazier

CHAPTER 15

OUTSIDE DURANGO

Malcolm, Rolf, and Angus were jarred awake by the conductor's call: "Durango! Arriving Durango!"

The train lurched to a stop. They stepped off into the early morning chill along with a dozen other passengers.

It was only a two-block walk to the sheriff's office where Sheriff Albert Smith was waiting. After exchanging pleasantries he opened the conversation. "I got your wire after they fixed the lines but the train had already made its' stop here and pulled out again. However, the depot agent said a heavy casket accompanied by what he thought was a Chinaman, was unloaded here. A buckboard picked it up right away but no one saw where it went. Me and my men have combed the town but can't find no trace of it. Jist what is the story, anyway? It sounds awful fishy."

"You bet it's fishy," Rolf responded. "Incidentally, before I start, here's my temporary U. S. Marshal's appointment. Just wanted you to know that we're doing everything according to the book here."

"Yeah, that's OK. I knew about that and it ain't no problem. We'll cooperate. I'm real short of manpower what with all the miners and cowboys in town, but we'll help any way we can."

"Fine," Rolf said, visibly relieved that his authority wouldn't be challenged. "Now let me tell you why we're here and what we know about the people we're lookin' for."

It only took a few minutes to tell the story.

Sheriff Smith just shook his head. "That's the darndest tale I ever heard. If you boys weren't settin' right here I doubt if I'd believe a word of it! But I know one thing fer sure. The Chinese criminals are gettin' mighty active around here. We

89

hear that they are shaking down the local Chinese, the businessmen who operate laundries and restaurants. Probably extorting money, protection money, out of them. The Chinese don't complain to us and the tongs haven't messed around with the general population. So we haven't had a problem. Of course we never had a murder and kidnapping so I reckon we'd better get to work."

He glanced sideways at Malcolm and continued, "If the lady wasn't married to your business partner, I doubt if anyone would get too interested in the situation. Chinese problems don't get much attention around here."

"I know that," Malcolm replied. "They're treated like dirt by just about everyone. But, I'll guarantee you one thing. You've never met better people than Su Chang and her husband. If you can't get people to help us, we'll mount a search on our own!"

"Don't go off half cocked, Malcolm. I didn't say we wouldn't help you. We will. Now, what we need to consider is this. Since we haven't seen any sign of any of them in town, I figure they loaded the casket on a buckboard and headed either straight to California, if that's where their headquarters is, or, and I favor this idea, they're hidin' out in an old mine shaft or cabin up in the mountains around here. There's a lot of places to look. I could deputize a bunch of men but they'd make a lot of racket. Some fool always gets trigger-happy and somebody gets shot just about every time we send a posse out. I think we should go out quietly, just two small parties of us, and search the countryside. That way we avoid a lot of confusion and we'll be totally in control of the situation. What do you think?"

"Sounds good to me," Rolf offered, pleased with the take charge attitude of the sheriff. "You're probably right and they're holed up around here somewhere. If they were goin' straight to California, they would've stayed on that train. The question is, why would they bring Su Chang here, anyway? It doesn't add up, but not much in this case does."

"Yeah, it may be awhile before we get the answer to that one. Maybe they just wanted to lay over here for a few days until the heat dies down, maybe for several months, then slip out and either catch a train to California, or go out on horseback. I don't know, but I've got a deputy I can leave in charge here. Why don't I get a couple of my boys and we'll start lookin'?" Smith pointed on his map to a large area on the east side of town. "You three work the west side. We'll take the east. If you spot 'em, hold your fire and come and get us. That way all six of us will be together if there's any gunplay. We'll do the same if we spot 'em first."

"How about horses?" Malcolm asked. "Have you got any to spare?"

"I'll have three mares in short order that are used to mountain trails and we'll get some food," Albert said, and nodded to a deputy. "All you need to bring is your rifles and bedrolls. It gets plenty cold. Also, we need to get together every night. No need for us all to be stumblin' around in the dark."

The deputy returned with the horses and food. They wasted no time in leaving town. Within an hour they were high in the mountains and the two groups split up as planned.

Malcolm, Rolf, and Angus followed the first old mining trail they came across, figuring it would lead them to abandoned shafts or cabins. Stealth was their major concern. Not a word passed until after about an hours' climb up the torturous trail, Rolf raised his hand and whispered, "Mine shaft."

Quietly they dismounted in a stand of tall aspens that rose next to a tiny mountain stream. Each man allowed his animal to drink, then hobbled them to graze contentedly in the tall grass.

Rolf said he would approach from the left, Malcolm was come in from the right, and Angus was to crawl up on top of the shaft, just over the entrance.

Tall grass was the only cover available. To avoid detection they would have to crawl some two hundred yards to the entrance.

"Wagon tracks," Angus whispered.

Malcolm and Rolf covered the distance on their bellies and

Ernest C. Frazier

waited until Angus was in position. Rolf gave the hands-down signal to Malcolm to stay put and whispered, "Cover me." Malcolm laid his rifle barrel across a boulder and trained it on the entrance to the shaft. Rolf dropped to his belly and slipped inside. He re-emerged in a couple of minutes and told Angus to come back down.

"The mine is caved in. I could only get in a few yards. Nobody's in there. But, it looks like we're hot on their trail. Look at this." He held up a ladies' oriental scarf made of the finest silk.

"Su Chang's no dummy," Malcolm said as he examined the article. "She's leavin' us a trail and we aren't far behind. They only had a one-day head start. One of us had better ride over and get Albert and his boys. We may need all the help we can get."

"From up on top, I could see where the wagon came up to the entrance," Angus chimed in. "Then the tracks went back out and joined the trail. They must've made a quick stop here, saw it wasn't fit to hide in and headed on."

"OK," Rolf was thinking out loud, "Malcolm, why don't you go round up Albert and his boys? Angus and I will keep on the trail. If we find 'em, we'll wait for you before we start any action."

"I figure it will take two or three hours before we get back here," Malcolm calculated.

"Right," Rolf replied. "We'll keep movin' and see if we can't get 'em in our sights. Tell Albert we're on the right track. And, good luck to you. If you get into any problems just fire three shots in the air. We'll find you."

"Maybe you'd better do the same if you get in a jam," Malcolm said. "Things could heat up pretty fast. Well, I'm goin'. See you later." He started back down the trail while Rolf and Angus pressed on.

Over the next three hours, they located several abandoned mine shafts and a couple of dilapidated cabins. They found nothing until they got to the second cabin. They found fresh

92

tracks and could see that someone had sat in the dust-covered chairs. A few breadcrumbs and a small chunk of cheese were on the floor, as yet undisturbed by rodents.

"How many do you reckon were here?" Rolf asked.

"I can't tell," Angus answered. "Might have been three or more. I just don't know. But it looks like we're closin' in. They're probably a few hours ahead of us. Maybe just a few minutes."

Invigorated by their findings, they moved on, snaking higher and higher into the mountains. As dusk closed in, they found a level spot among the tall pines to pitch camp. No fires were lit and conversation was held to a whisper.

"I wonder what's keeping Malcolm?" Angus asked. "It's been about three hours since he left. Hope they get here before dark."

"We are here," a quiet voice came from behind, causing Angus' hand to drop for his six-shooter. Then he paused and grinned sheepishly with the realization that Malcolm and Albert's group had infiltrated the camp.

While the men ate a cold supper, Rolf told them about the areas that he and Angus had explored.

"Look at this map. We're about right here. This old trail takes you to Mesa Verde. It's about a two or three day ride."

"What is Mesa Verde? I never heard of it," Angus asked.

"Abandoned ruins where ancient Indians lived. Huge cliff dwellings down in the canyons and a lot of caves high up on the cliffs. Several thousand feet high. Cowboys discovered the ruins awhile back and a lot of it hasn't been explored yet. You could hide hundreds of people in that area. It covers a lot of miles."

"I've heard of the place," Malcolm said. "If they got into that area, what would be our chances of finding them?"

"Pretty slim. If I wanted to hide someone real bad, and I was this close to Mesa Verde, that's exactly where I'd go."

Ted and Hank, Albert's deputies, had been quiet up to this point. Hank broke the silence, "If you had enough food and water, y'all could hole up there all winter and no one could get to you. I've been up there a few times. The snow gets ten to twenty feet deep. We'd better to get to 'em quick or we'll never find 'em."

Malcolm said, "My guess is they think they've made a clean get-a-way and figure that everyone is lookin' for Su Chang in St. Louis. Of course, if they've been watchin' the trail, they may have seen us and know better. Regardless, they're running for their lives. I reckon they'll keep Su Chang alive after going to all the trouble to kidnap her. You're right. We need to find 'em quick. We'd better get a good nights' sleep and head to Mesa Verde in the morning. What do you think?"

The response was unanimous. The logic pointed them toward Mesa Verde.

"Ted," Albert turned to his deputy, "We'll need a lot more supplies before this trip is over. Head back to town and pick up a couple hundred feet of rope so we can make ladders. For food get twenty pounds of jerky and a sack of beans. Better get some flapjack flour, molasses, hard tack, and probably five pounds of coffee. Charge it to the county. If Dutch Schmidt will bring his pack mules out, we could sure use 'em. He knows these mountains and the mules are good in the high country. Tell him I'll deputize him and he'll get full pay for him and his animals."

Angus handed some money to Ted. "Here's a dollar. Might bring back a can of pipe tobacco and a box of matches for me and spend the rest on hard candy for all of us. We might need a little sugar before this trip is done."

"Anybody else need anything? Albert inquired. No one responded so he finished his instructions. "Ted, we'll probably be clear to Mesa Verde before you get back from town. You know where the trail forks, one trail going on up to the rim and the other down to the canyon? We'll either be there to meet you, or you'll see a written message nailed to a tree tellin' you where we are."

"I'll find you," Ted replied as he swung his leg over the saddle. "Adios!"

CHAPTER 16

NOGALES, MEXICO

Levi rode out of Tucson with no way of knowing that he was living out the last days of his life, blissfully unaware that he'd been betrayed by the very man he'd put the most confidence in, Jed the assay agent. His thoughts were on the lonely miles of desert he'd have to cover on his way back to the mine. He was in no hurry to return to the world of backbreaking labor, felt a strong need for a little excitement, and decided to see some of the world he'd heard about but never experienced. He headed straight south to Nogales, a roaring border town with one leg in the United States and the other in Mexico. He planned to spend a night there, then swing east for the three-day ride to Ft. Huachuca. From there it would only be another two days ride to the Chiricahua Mountains and the copper mine.

It took two days to get to the border. He watered his horses at a public trough on the U. S. side and pondered his next move. He knew that Mexican border towns were dangerous places so he stalled around for a while, wondering if he really wanted to cross into Mexico. He watched the people moving through the port of entry which was nothing more than a sentry box manned by a pair of unshaven, Mexican soldiers in filthy cotton uniforms. He saw no delays as a thin stream of humanity, pausing only to press pesos or dollars into a sentry's hand, trickled across the border. Knowing he would regret it forever if he didn't take advantage of the opportunity, he gathered his nerve, approached, and requested permission to cross over. The sentry stood mute for a moment and Levi wondered if he could understand English. His answered came, when, still silent, the man extended his hand, palm up. Levi handed him a silver dollar and was motioned through.

His jaw dropped as he rode down the dusty streets of Nogales. He'd heard of the poverty but he was unprepared for what he saw--open meat markets featuring freshly skinned goats and chickens hanging upside down. Their blood drained into the street and flies swarmed over the warm carcasses. He recoiled, his stomach tightening as the stench of decaying meat filled his nostrils. Street urchins besieged him, clamoring for money or offering to find him a bargain on anything from cheap trinkets to women or whiskey or anything else the sprawling, smelly, vibrant city had to offer. Merchants were hawking their wares from storefronts, tents, alleys, ox carts, and any other location that was available. Saloons, gambling dens, cantinas, and brothels were running full blast even though it was only late afternoon. He had never seen such a display of aggressive salesmanship in his life.

One clean cut young boy did get his attention by telling him that for one dollar he would take him to a fine restaurant and hotel. "All the Gringos go there. They import fresh meat, water, and liquor every day from the north." Also, the boy offered to guard his horse and wagon throughout the night even though they would be parked in the livery stable in back of the hotel. Levi took him up on the arrangement and paid him twenty-five cents down with a promise to pay the other seventy-five cents in the morning. The boy, whose name was Pedro, agreed, and led Levi to the Hotel Americana De Norte, located just one block off the main street.

"I'll check in and you can take my rig around back. I'm going to get something to eat then I'll come down and see how you are doing," Levi was still a bit apprehensive at leaving the young boy in charge, but he didn't see any alternatives if he wanted to spend the night in comfort. "Do you want me to bring you a sandwich or something?"

"Si, Senor. I had nothing to eat all day," Pedro's black eyes lit up in anticipation. "We are very poor since Papa lost the farm."

"Where is your family?" Levi felt a bit of concern for the skinny boy.

"Papa died last year. Mama and my two sisters, Rosa and Carmen work down the street at that cantina." He pointed a block south. Levi saw a large, adobe building with a sign saying: CASA BLANCA

"Looks like a busy place," Levi observed as steady pedestrian traffic entered the establishment. "What do they do there?"

Pedro looked at the ground and scuffed a bare toe in the dirt, obviously uncomfortable at having to reply. "Mama tends bar. Rosa and Carmen work in the back rooms."

"I see," Levi didn't want to push the matter further at that moment. "I'll go on in and eat. I'll bring you somethin' pretty soon. Take good care of that rig!"

The hotel was neat and clean and sported an excellent restaurant. His steak was cooked medium, just like he ordered, with fried potatoes and fresh baked bread spread with home churned butter. When he finished, he ordered a beefsteak sandwich for Pedro. For some reason the boy fascinated him and he felt his story would be an interesting one. He didn't have anyone else to talk to and hoped Pedro would show him around.

Levi watched with amusement, then with some pity, as the sandwich disappeared in a few bites. "Boy, we need to get some fat on you. How often do you get something to eat, anyway?"

"Sometimes, when the Casa Blanca closes in the morning, if there is any food left, Mama will slip some to me. Sometimes there isn't any so I go out and try to earn money to buy food."

"Don't your Mama and sisters earn enough to feed all of you?"

"They don't get to keep hardly no money," once again Pedro was stabbing the ground with his toes.

"I guess I don't understand. Why is that?" Levis asked, thoroughly ignorant in the ways business was conducted in Mexico.

"Senor, my Papa had a small farm. The drought came and

we had no rain. The beans and the squash and the corn, they all died. We didn't have no money so Papa borrowed money from Don Diego. No crops came the next year so Papa couldn't pay. He got the heart attack and died out in the bean field when Don Diego's men came to collect the money."

"Tell me, Pedro. Just who is Don Diego?"

"He is a rich man. He owns a giant hacienda here. Anyone who rents land from him has to sell him their cattle. So, he controls the cattle prices. He's got the freight lines, the newspaper, this hotel, the Casa Blanca, and, the Casa Azul. I don't know what all he owns but he is the richest man in town."

"Pedro, are you telling me that you sisters and your mother are forced to work at the Casa Blanca to pay off that farm debt?"

"Si."

"How long will it take to work off the debt?"

"Three years."

"How old are your sisters?"

"They are twins. They are fifteen."

Levi let that information soak in for a while, then asked, "I suppose there are other women working in there?"

"Probably thirty or more. They came from farms or businesses that went broke. And that's just in the Casa Blanca. Don Diego has more in his other businesses and the hacienda. The vacqueros that run the cattle, they all owe him money, and don't get no wages. Just room and board."

"Well, I ain't got nothin' to do around here tonight. Suppose we go over to the Casa Blanca. I'd just like to look around. I never been in a place like that. But I don't want nobody bothering me. Will they let you in there?"

"Senor, I go in there all the time. I'll just tell Mama that no one is to bother us. We can set there all night as long as you buy a drink once in awhile."

"One other thing. Can I carry my .44 in there?"

"Senor, everybody carries a gun down here."

Levi checked his rig one more time, then they walked down to the cantina.

"Ask your Mama if she's got any good beer. I don't want no Mexican rotgut," Levi handed the boy a quarter as they entered.

Pedro spoke to his mother in Spanish. She smiled at Levi, handed Pedro a bottle, and motioned them to a table across the room.

Moments later, she was relieved by another bartender and came over to their table. Pedro introduced his mother, "Senor, this is my Mama. Her name is Lupe."

Levi stood up and offered her a chair.

Pedro, still speaking Spanish, told her of Levi's concern about their situation.

"Ask your Mama how much money it would take to pay off Don Diego so she and the girls could get loose from him," Levi instructed.

Pedro asked the question.

"She don't know for sure. It is a lot of money."

"I need to get back to the bar," Lupe, to Levi's surprise, excused herself in remarkably good English. "Don Diego is expected in here tonight. He always comes on Wednesday night."

"Wait a minute," said Levi. "I want to meet him when he comes in. Maybe you can introduce us."

Lupe frowned. She looked at Levi's .44 and lapsed back into Spanish.

"Pedro, tell your friend that Don Diego has many bodyguards and he had better not start any trouble."

Pedro interpreted.

Levi just laughed and said, "I ain't no gun slinger. I just want to talk to him about a straight up business deal. That's all. I ain't going to start no trouble down here. I'd get killed or land in jail in a minute and I know it."

The woman was visibly relieved.

She switched to English. "Just don't pull your gun, Senor. They will kill you." With that, she returned to the bar.

A Mariachi band began to play and they sat back to enjoy the music. Every once in awhile one of the girls working in the back would come out to pick up a drink or some food. They knew that Pedro was the little brother of Carmen and Rosa. They would swing by the table and run their fingers through his hair and joke with him a bit. But, none of them approached Levi. Evidently Lupe had put out the word.

Liquor was flowing freely. Soon everyone was treated to the spectacle of a well-inebriated Gringo cowboy jumping up on a table in an attempt to perform the Mexican Hat Dance. He failed miserably. As his feet pounded the table, it abruptly turned over and sent him crashing to the floor. Nobody was hurt and the band played on.

Rosa and Carmen came by to meet Pedro's new friend. Levi offered them a seat but they declined, saying they were busy. He noticed that the girls were very tired but doing their best to be cheerful. Neither was well developed. They were dressed in gaudy red dresses, cut low to display their modest cleavage, styled for women twice their age. They both reeked of cheap perfume and wore bright red lipstick in an effort to enhance their childish beauty.

"How do like workin' here?" Levi opened with a question.

The girls shrugged their shoulders and opened their hands, palms up, in a gesture of resignation. "What else can we do, Senor?" asked Rosa. "Don Diego owns us for three more years."

Levi could feel nothing but pity for them. "Maybe I can help," he said.

The band stopped playing. All conversation halted and the girls beat a hasty retreat back to their rooms. Don Diego, recognizable in his sparkling white linen suit topped with a panama straw was entering the room. He was armed with matching pistols that rested in white cowhide holsters. His feet were encased in black, custom cut boots. Two gunmen flanked him, each wearing a bandoleer of cartridges across his chest. One carried a .45 caliber Mexican army pistol--the other a .30-.30 carbine. Huge sombreros dwarfed their heads. They wore the uniform of Mexican vaqueros, complete with chaps and hand made boots with massive spurs. Each had a thick, drooping mustache and a weeks' growth of beard. Neither had bathed for days.

Don Diego was tall for a Mexican, immaculately clean, slender and quite handsome with long pomaded hair and a thin, waxed, mustache. He nodded at the bandleader and the music resumed. Everyone relaxed. Conversations were continued as Don Diego and his men seated themselves at his private table.

The place was rapidly filling with patrons, many of whom began to dance with the bar girls. Across the room, Levi saw that Don Diego was enjoying his dinner with a bottle of tequila. As though on parade, the most beautiful girls stopped at his table, seemingly to pay homage as he ate. He smiled and exchanged pleasantries with each one. They stayed briefly, then moved on.

When everyone had finished eating, Levi said, "Pedro, see if your mother will take me over and introduce me to Don Diego. I want to meet him."

The boy ran over, spoke to Lupe, then returned. "Senor, she is afraid to take you to Don Diego. She thinks there might be trouble. She won't come. She says you can talk to him. He can talk English."

"Well, I guess I can't blame her. Looks like I'll just have to go over and introduce myself. You stay here," Levi patted the boy on the head and left the table.

He sauntered over to Don Diego's table, making sure his hands were far away from his pistol, and said, "Howdy, I'm new in town but I hear you own this place and I wanted to meet you. In fact I may have a business proposition. Do you mind if I sit down?"

Levi startled himself at his own audacity, having spoken so boldly. He couldn't help but notice the bodyguard's hands hovering over their weapons as they waited for the reply. He tried to swallow but his mouth was dry.

Don Diego smiled a thin smile and motioned Levi to a chair. "My house is your house. What is your name, Senor?"

Levi told him his name and took a seat.

101

"I'll get right down to business," Levi said. "I've met Lupe, your bartender, and her two daughters. I know they're working off a debt and I can understand that. I'm just curious. How much cash money would it take to pay off the debt? I don't have a lot now but it's possible I could come up with the money in a few months."

Their eyes met for the first time. Levi saw no personality, no compassion, only a rattlesnake-like stare, that of a cunning predator. His own gaze withered and he glanced away, realizing that, regardless of his words, Don Diego was a man without a soul or a conscience.

"Senor, I am a man of honor. All I ask is the amount owed me. It would take three thousand American dollars if you pay by the end of the year. That's six months away." Don Diego spoke with the confidence of one who always makes the rules.

"What if I can't raise the money that soon?" asked Levi.

"Then we'll just have to see. My offer is good for six months."

"I've got partners in a mining operation up north. Can we draw up a paper with your offer? That way, if something ever happened to and they showed up with the money, the deal would still be good. Mining's a dangerous business as you probably know," Levi explained.

"No problem, Senor. I am a man of my word. Lupe! Bring me a sheet of paper and a pen and ink. Senor, I can read English so you can write out the agreement for both of us to sign," Don Diego was in a garrulous mood as the tequila warmed his body. He also was more interested in the money than the women. Women were easy to come by. Money was a different matter.

"Well, I ain't much good at writin'," explained Levi, not wanting to actually admit he could neither read nor write. "Can we get someone else to write it up?"

"I'll do it," Don Diego responded. "It will only take a minute." He wrote a few lines and read them back to Levi. He agreed to the content and they signed the document.

Levi thanked Don Diego, shook hands with him, pocketed the paper and returned to his table where Pedro was waiting.

"I'm ready to go back to the hotel and get some sleep. How about you? Are you goin' to sleep in the stables with my rig?" Levi asked.

"I will sleep in the wagon. No one will bother any of your things." Pedro assured him. "Senor," he added, "two Gringo cowboys came to the table while you were talking to Don Diego. They asked me where you were staying but I told them I didn't know."

"Are they still in here?" Levi asked.

Pedro looked around. "There they go. They are just walking out the door." He pointed as Levi strained to see through the crowd.

"Huh," he said, seeing only their backs, "they look a little like a couple of hombres I ate with at a hotel in Tucson. I don't know why they'd want to know about me. Did they say anything else?"

"All they asked was where you were staying."

"Tell you what, Pedro, is there a rear exit out of here?"

"Si, Senor, we can slip out the back if you want to."

"Might be a good idea. Let's get out of here. I don't like the sound of those boys lookin' for me. They ain't up to any good."

In the alley, a group of men had gathered around some tables. Lighting was provided by kerosene lanterns. Some were playing cards. Others were just loafing and smoking.

Levi asked, "Who are all of those people and why're they out here playin' cards?"

Pedro replied, "They are the husbands and fathers of the women working inside. They are waiting to take them home when they get off work."

Levi shook his head, finding the whole thing unimaginable.

They easily avoided scrutiny as they made their way in the darkened alley back to the hotel. Levi cursed softly as they slipped in slime and filth, refuse thrown out by housewives and merchants who never considered burning or burying their garbage.

"I've got to wash off my boots before I go in," Levi said, pulling off his boots at the watering trough. "I'll see you at the stables in the morning."

Across the street, the two Gringo gunmen stood in the darkened doorway of an abandoned shop, observing every move that Levi made.

CHAPTER 17

THE CAVE

Su Chang slept through the stop in Trinidad. Halfway to Durango, she began to stir. Dao Chi sensed her movements, opened the casket and administered another dose of chloroform, assuring that she would be asleep when they arrived.

A wagon and two tongsmen met the train in Durango and loaded the casket onto the wagon. Dao Chi climbed aboard and they rode out of town immediately.

Su Chang, still in the casket, awakened to the sounds of their conversation. It lead her to believe that she was to be hidden in the Durango area until any search parties tired of looking for her. Later, they planned to take her to San Francisco to the house of Kai Mang. She concluded that the stop in Durango was for strategic reasons. Once telegraph service was restored, the news of her abduction would cause the authorities to halt and search the train at its next stop. That would certainly lead to her discovery.

Secondly, the presence of the tong in Durango provided the people to assist in transporting her to a hiding place.

She could hear her captors speaking of Mesa Verde, a place unknown to her, as their destination.

Their first stop was at an abandoned mine where she was allowed leave the casket and move around a bit. A quick look at the two men helping Dao Chi gave her little hope for relief. She could tell they were nothing more than poor coolies, sent to do Dao Chi's bidding, and would undoubtedly obey his orders without question. They only stayed a few minutes as the shaft was caved in a few yards from the entrance. Su Chang was the last one to step out of the mine. Unbeknownst to the others, she dropped a silk scarf as she left.

Dao Chi ordered the coolies to carry the empty casket to a deep gulch, several hundred yards past the mine, drop it to the bottom and throw enough branches on top to cover it from view.

Su Chang would no longer be traveling as a corpse, but she wasn't quite ready for Dao Chi's next move. As she seated herself at his command in the back of the wagon, he hobbled her ankles with a chain.

"You won't be running away. If you should shout or scream, we will gag you." Dao Chi pulled out a sizeable length of dirty cloth and held it up to her face. "You will sit quietly!"

Su Chang nodded mutely.

The wagon contained a substantial supply of food, blankets, rope and water, causing her to reason that the plan was to hide out for a long time. The driver put the whip to the horses, evidently fearing they would be pursued. She was doubly pleased that she had left her telltale scarf behind.

It was a bone-jarring ride of two days before they pulled into a spectacular area of cliffs, canyons, caves, and ruins, an area so vast it could hide several armies. Su Chang marveled at the spectacle and could see why they'd come to Mesa Verde.

"What is this place?" she asked.

"Indians lived here in the past. They left this place many years ago," Dao Chi explained.

They camped that night high at the edge of a steep cliff. Looking down, one could see that it was a thousand feet or more to the canyon floor below. Su Chang reeled back from the dizzying height and refused to look down.

In the morning, much to her dismay, the plan of concealment became clear. About fifty yards down on the face of the cliff was the perfect cave dwelling. The only way to enter from the top would be to lower oneself down on ropes or ladders, a dangerous maneuver but the only option for that approach. Coming up from the bottom appeared to be impossible due to the sheer rock face of the cliff. Su Chang could see, that once they were safely in the cave and their ropes and ladders were put out of sight, they would probably never be detected by anyone.

Down below, the canyon floor offered miles of major ruins and easily accessed caves which they have chosen to could hide in. But Su Chang understood the mindset of her captors. They would do anything within their power to avoid detection, and the high cliff was the perfect place for them.

In the morning they gagged Su Chang, chained her ankle to the wagon wheel, constructed a rope ladder, and began the laborious task of lowering their supplies down to the cave. This took most of the morning. When finished, they released her.

Dao Chi said, "Crawl down the ladder and get in the cave."

She looked down and her head spun. She reeled back and tried to collapse on the ground. Dao Chi grabbed her, propped her up, and scored her back with a thrust of his dagger. She screamed and turned to face her tormentor, her eyes pleading for mercy. He spun her around, hit her with his riding crop, and said, "Go now or we will throw the sack over your head and carry you down!"

She took a deep breath, summoned her courage, grabbed the ladder and forced one leg over the precipice. She focused her eyes straight ahead, and, as though crawling through wet cement, inched her way down to the cave.

Once inside, her body wouldn't stop trembling. When she finally looked around the cave, she was pleased with its layout. It consisted of a large chamber connected to a smaller one that she could crawl into, assuring her a measure of privacy. She knew they might be there a long time and wanted to keep to herself as much as possible.

Dao Chi stayed on top of the rim to dispose of the wagon. He drove it along the canyon edge for about three miles. Observing no one in the canyon, he believed that he and his companions were alone and hid the wagon in some heavy brush. The horses posed another problem. There would be no way to care for them now. New horses could be acquired when the time was right, but, for now, he couldn't have them drawing attention. He looked a thousand feet down and saw a stand of timber. He unharnassed the animals, put bridles on, led them to the edge of the cliff and tried to drive them over the side. They balked and tried to back up. He drew his pistol and shot them in the head. They plunged headlong to the canyon floor.

Su Chang and the coolies were startled to hear shots echoing against the canyon walls. They looked at each other.

"Why is Dao Chi shooting his gun?" Su Chang asked.

The coolies shrugged their shoulders.

"Maybe it's not his gun. Maybe somebody is shooting at him," Su Chang speculated.

Her comment upset the coolies. They pulled out their daggers, a signal that she would die if Dao Chi failed to return. She would only hinder their efforts to escape.

They could only wait for Dao Chi's return, if indeed he was to return.

Dao Chi saw no movement in the canyon. *Good*, he thought. *No one heard those shots.*

But he was wrong. The search party, having pushed their horses all night, were pulling into the canyon.

"Gunshots!" Albert's deputy, Hank, exclaimed, his eyes widening.

"Do tell," Albert chided. "Don't you think the rest of us might have figured that out?"

"You don't suppose the tong fired those shots?" Malcolm asked. "They can't be far ahead but I can't believe they'd risk giving their position away."

"Maybe it is them," Albert answered. "They probably figger we're two days behind. 'Course the way those shots echo around the canyon, nobody can tell where they came from. Maybe they shot a deer or come up on some poor fool's camp and decided to put 'im away. Why don't we leave a message here for Ted and Dutch and split up like before. One party takes the high rim and the others stay down here."

"Let's do it," Rolf said. "Who wants to take the high country?"

It was agreed that Rolf, Malcolm, and Angus would take the trail to the top. Albert and Hank would work the canyon.

"What's the best way to contact each other? We don't want any shootin' goin' on now." Malcolm asked, then answered his own question. "Maybe we could use smoke."

They agreed that three puffs of smoke followed a minute later by three more puffs would be their signal to get together.

"Ted'll bring in the additional supplies. Tomorrow, if we haven't signaled, one of you better come down and pick up some grub. It'll take several days to search that rim and your grub won't hold out. We'll have plenty of it," Albert advised.

They muffled their horses' hooves with strips of cloth. Any noise would surely cause their quarry to either move out before them, or, if cornered, use Su Chang as a human shield while negotiating their escape.

Dao Chi returned and climbed down to the cave.

Su Chang was relieved to see the coolies putting their daggers away. Only Dao Chi could keep the tongsmen in line.

That night, she slept in the back chamber and the men slept close to the entrance. There was no way she could exit without their knowledge.

As she lay quietly on her blankets, she overheard bits and pieces of their conversation--talk that caused her blood to freeze.

Dao Chi told the coolies that, if they were hunted down and faced capture, their lives would be worth nothing. They would try to shoot their way out, using Su Chang as a shield. If that failed they were to throw her off the cliff. He told them that by doing so they would save face--and maybe their lives if they escaped--by not allowing her to be returned to her husband. He said that Kai Mang had been specific in his instruction that Ben Wang was never to see his wife again, no matter what price must be paid!

Ernest C. Frazier

CHAPTER 18

MASSACRE AT ROSE PIT MINE

Levi ate a quick breakfast at the hotel, checked out, and took a platter of hot cakes out to the stables for Pedro. He found him asleep in the wagon. After a quick good bye, he left the boy setting on a milk stool devouring the food and rode up to the border crossing. He had no trouble exiting Mexico and within a few minutes was back on the trail to the mine. It was a beautiful morning in the desert, a bit chilly but the sun soon solved that problem. He was worried about the two gunslingers. He kept his eyes open but didn't see anyone on his trail and assumed they lost him in Nogales.

He made it to Ft. Huachuca in three days and asked the sentries at the main gate if they had seen a pair of cowboys in the area recently. They hadn't.

Dinner was being served in the non-commissioned officers mess. An old Master Sergeant asked Levi to eat with them, an invitation accepted without hesitation.

He enjoyed an hour of food and conversation with the cavalrymen.

His host had to return to duty right after the meal so Levi rode back to the main gate with him, thanked him for the hospitality, and rode out of the fort.

"Say," one of the troopers said, "I did see a couple of cowboys ride by right after you went to eat. But they didn't come into the fort. They just kept on going east."

"Did you get a good look at them?" Levi inquired.

"Nope. They were about a quarter of a mile away but they looked like cowboys to me."

"Thanks," said Levi. "I'll keep an eye out for them."

That night, he piled up some pillows and blankets in the

111

wagon so it would look like he was sleeping there. Then, he slipped off in the dark with his bedroll and climbed to the top of a butte.

The night passed without incident and he was embarrassed by his fear. *Probably those cowboys the soldier saw work on a ranch around here and I'm worryin' a lot about nothin'.*

He left early in the morning. It would only take a few hours to the mine. As the day wore on he relaxed a bit. The trail behind revealed nothing and he was anxious to see his dad and brother.

Another rider was approaching the mine from the north and would be arriving at about his same time.

Peg Leg Charlie, the old prospector and former sidekick of Smooth Mouth Sam, was making good on his promise to look up Smooth Mouth and get the whole story regarding the branding incident. Peg Leg led two donkeys laden with prospecting tools, tent, grub, a wooden barrel of water, bedroll, clothing, a .38 caliber six shooter, and, ammunition. He hadn't seen a soul on the trail for almost a month. While he enjoyed solitude most of the time, he was anxious to see Smooth Mouth and his boys and enjoy some friendly conversation.

As evening approached, he topped a rise. It revealed the long, sloping valley he was looking for. He was within a mile of the mine and he could make out the shaft entrance from his vantage point.

To his right he could see a wagon laden with supplies approaching from the east.

Probably Smooth Mouth or one of the boys, been out shopping. Maybe bringing in some fresh grub.

He paused to pour a bucket of water for his animals. He attention was diverted by a movement in a deep gully that ran alongside the wagon trail. He could see two horsemen making their way along out of sight of the wagon. They made no attempt to come up onto the trail. To Peg Leg, it was obvious they did not want to be seen.

At that moment, Smooth Mouth and Hitch came out of the mine following a cart loaded with ore.

"Looka there!," Hitch hollered, pointing to the wagon lumbering toward them less than a half mile away. "Levi's finally makin' it back. I'm goin' to kick his rump until he tells me what took him so long! I'm flat starved for some decent food!"

"What the devil?" Smooth Mouth interrupted. "Who're those riders comin' up out of the gulch?"

Levi also spotted them. *The gunslingers!* He was only three hundred yards from the mine. He stood up in the wagon and swung his bullwhip like a man possessed. His animals charged ahead, straining against the weight of the wagon. But it was no race. In a matter of seconds, the gunslingers were riding neck to neck beside his team. They drew their pistols and yelled at him to pull over.

Smooth Mouth and Hitch stood like they were nailed to the ground. The sight of the guns finally galvanized them into action. They dropped their tools and raced to the mine shack to get their weapons.

On the bluff, Peg Leg could only watch. Levi ignored the command, grabbed his rifle, reined the team hard to the left and set the brake. The top-heavy wagon crashed over and skidded on its' side. He cleared the seat while the wheels were still spinning and fell on his belly. Shielded by the wreckage, he bellowed the alarm, "Claim jumpers! Claim jumpers!"

The gunslingers were on him in a second, circling him like a wounded coyote, trying to get a decent shot. He rolled in the dirt, trying to get to the wagon but his panicked horses, struggling to jerk away from their harnesses, were dragging it away. He tried to run but a slug from a .44 splintered his ankle. He fell, rolled to a prone position, and triggered off two rounds. The first shot sent Sy's hat spiraling skyward. Two inches lower would have blown his brains out. The second shot went wild as Bob opened fire, sending three rounds into Levi's body.

Peg Leg cursed himself for not carrying a rifle as the carnage unfolded. He was way out of pistol range, and, with only one functional leg, he would have a hard time getting close enough to fire without being detected. He watched helplessly, tears flooding his eyes as he watched Levi go limp.

Leaving Levi to die in the dust, Bob and Sy gave their horses full rein. They pressed the attack, charging the mine where Smooth Mouth and Hitch, now armed, were running for cover behind the ore cart. Sy's first round, fired from his rifle at a full gallop, caught Smooth Mouth in the hip. Hitch heard the scream of pain and saw his father's leg shoot out from under him. He abandoned the protection of the cart and raced out to help Smooth Mouth who flopped about like a rag doll in his struggle to get back on his feet.

Grabbing him with his left arm, Hitch fired point blank at a rider who was closing in fast.

The slug hit Bob at the top of his left shoulder, knocking him out of the saddle. With pulverizing force, he landed flat on his back. His momentum sent him rocketing down the slope, free-wheeling like a bobsled. Hitch and Smooth Mouth lurched to the side in an attempt to avoid the human projectile, a futile effort as he crashed into their legs, sending them tumbling like tenpins.

Disoriented, they struggled to get to their feet.

Peg Leg watched in horror as Sy emptied his rifle into his friends. They fell without so much as a whimper.

When the slaughter was finished, Sy dismounted to attend to his wounded companion.

Peg Leg saw the distraction. Wanting to hear the conversation between the outlaws, he decided to take a chance. He hobbled and muzzled his donkeys. He couldn't have them braying or wandering around. Abundant cover was provided by a heavy stand of mesquite and various cacti ranging from scraggly ocotillo to the giant saguaro.

Sliding like a snake through the brush, he made it to a dry watering trough. He was dangerously close and began to have second thoughts. *This ain't the smartest thing I ever did. I can't do a thing now to save Smooth Mouth and the boys.* However, he was within earshot of the two killers and couldn't back out if he wanted to. He sneaked a look around the end of the trough and saw Bob, still on the ground, shaking out the cobwebs from his tumble. Sy was probing his shoulder.

"I think the bullet glanced off your collarbone but you're bleedin' quite a bit," Sy was saying. "It don't look like there's any bullet in there, but I can't tell for sure. We're out of whiskey so there ain't no way I can sterilize it and I can't get you drunk to probe it. What do you want to do?"

"I'm hurtin'. I'm about half sick from that bullet wound and my leg and ribs must be cracked. I hit the ground awful hard and slidin' into them pert near killed me," Bob moaned. "You'd better get me to the Doc in Tombstone."

"Well, can you ride a horse? There ain't no way I can haul you in. Their wagon is smashed 'cause that knot head wrecked it and his horses stampeded."

"Yeah, I can ride. It'll hurt but it beats layin' out here waitin' for the buzzards."

Peg Leg, lying as still as a log, toyed a bit with the idea of trying to gun them down, a thought he soon discarded. His eyesight was bad and he'd never been in a gunfight. He knew if his first shot missed, and anything over twenty-five yards was a long shot for him, he wouldn't stand a chance against the two skilled gunmen.

Bob's gelding had not strayed far from the scene. He struggled to mount up, grinding his teeth in pain.

Peg Leg cringed and fought the impulse to draw his gun when Sy flipped his lasso around Smooth Mouth's feet and drug his body to the mineshaft. Then Levi and Hitch got the same treatment.

"Nobody ever comes around this part of the country, but I figure we'll keep 'em out of sight until we get back. It might take three or four days and I don't want the coyotes draggin' 'em around. We'll bury 'em then and there ain't a soul in the world will know where they are!" Sy, as unconcerned as if he were buring a dead calf, dismounted and rolled the mine cart up to block the mine's entrance.

"Coyotes may get in there, but they can't drag 'em out. Let's go get you patched up!"

Peg Leg breathed more freely as the two killers rode out of sight. Then he walked into the mine.

His first impulse was to start digging a grave. But he had a better thought. *If I bury the bodies, these hombres'll come back and see what's happened. They'll hightail it clear out of the country before I can get the law down here. If I leave the bodies alone, they won't suspect nothing. They'll bury 'em themselves and start workin' the mine.*

With that in mind, he dropped down and went through the pockets of each man to see if they had any personal belongings he could take care of. He found little more than well-worn wallets containing money, pocketknives, small change, and a few plugs of tobacco. Something in Levi's pocket caught his eye: An agreement dated in Nogales bearing the signatures of Levi and Don Diego.

He left the other items undisturbed but carefully folded the document and placed it in his pocket. Then he went up to the shack, which served as a bunkhouse and looked around. It was filthy and nothing of substance was found there except for a sheet of paper lying on a dynamite crate. The heading read: STOCK ASSIGNMENT. It was signed by Smooth Mouth and J. T. Smith.

Without touching another thing, Peg Leg placed that document in his pocket with the other one, uttered what he could remember of the Lord's prayer, and waived a sad farewell to his three friends. His donkeys were waiting when he got back up the hill.

CHAPTER 19

SEARCHING THE ANCIENT CITY

Deep in the canyon, Albert and Hank were beginning their search of the ruins. Hank had never been there before and was surprised to find himself searching an ancient city constructed inside a huge, cathedral like cavern. The living quarters were stacked on top of each other, bringing to mind the two and three story hotels he'd seen in Durango and other towns. A natural overhang, functioning like a giant stone canopy, was created by the cavern and provided excellent protection.

Creeping in silence they methodically searched each room, mindful to watch for rattlesnakes and scorpions that abounded in the rocks. As evening approached, they were treated to the sight of a half dozen large brown bears beside the stream that ran through the canyon. Their presence was something they hadn't considered. Common sense told them to avoid confrontation since they didn't want to fire their weapons. They gave them a wide berth.

"Do you suppose any of them have dens in the ruins?" Hank whispered to Albert as they stooped and cautiously entered another chamber.

"I don't know, but we're not doin' any searching at night, that's fer sure. Running into the Chinese would be tough enough without having to fight bears at the same time. Let's go back into one of the empty rooms and pitch camp there. We can't be lightin' any fires so we're stuck with cold jerky again. Good thing we brought enough blankets to keep us from freezin'. It gets right smart cold up here at night. I wonder how the boys are doin' up on the rim? I reckon they're gettin' ready to bed down," Albert speculated, unable to see any sign of their companions in the approaching gloom.

117

Rolf, Malcolm, and Angus were now at the top of the canyon's rim, a trip that took the entire day. They'd encountered no humans but had also observed several bears as they disappeared into the brush ahead. That night, they found a well wooded spot a few yards off the main trail and pitched their cold, dark camp.

The presence of the bears caused them to post guards in three-hour shifts.

No bears showed up so at daybreak they ate a breakfast of hard tack and jerky, washed it down with cold coffee and renewed the search.

They looked through every grove of timber, rock formation, and small cave they could find. It was exhaustive, tedious work. At the end of two days they had nothing to show for their efforts and still had many miles to go.

On the morning of the third day they saw white smoke coming from the canyon below. There were three puffs followed a minute later by three more.

"That's our signal," Rolf said. "The boys have found somethin'. Let's get back down there, pronto!"

At the bottom of the canyon two events had prompted Hank to send up the smoke signals. While Albert searched the ruins Hank went off the trail to look around. At the base of a cliff he found two horses lying dead in the heavy timber. He saw they'd been there only a short time, as rigor mortis hadn't set in. He was puzzled by the absence of hoof prints even though the ground was quite soft. He noticed they were draft horses, used for pulling wagons, and their harnesses had been removed.

It was a thousand feet or more to the top of the cliff. *Could they possibly have fallen from there?*

A closer look revealed that each of them had broken legs. What was more startling was the fact that both had been shot!

Without further speculation he left the scene and ran back to the ruins where Albert had been searching.

Seeing no one, he stopped for a minute and started to call out. Then he heard a moan. The sheriff, obviously in pain, was lying propped up against a boulder. Hank drew his pistol.

"Put your gun away," Albert croaked. "I'm havin' chest pains. Must be this altitude."

"Have you got heart trouble?" Hank asked as he holstered his weapon.

"Not that I know of, but I feel terrible. Better make some smoke and get the other boys back down here," Albert responded in a weak voice as he began writing in pain.

It took almost three hours for Rolf, Malcolm, and Angus to get back down into the canyon.

"He might be having a heart attack. He's having chest pains," Hank announced. "We've got to get him back to Durango but he sure can't ride no horse!"

"Well, maybe that problem is solving itself right now," said Angus as he pointed back up the trail. "Looks like Ted coming in the wagon with Dutch and his mules."

"Thank God!" Hank shouted as he ran up the trail to tell them to hurry up.

They all pitched in to unload the supplies, made a bed in the wagon out of blankets and loaded their distressed comrade in with a jug of water and some food.

They drew straws to see who would drive the wagon back to town. Hank got the short one.

He got up on the wagon, pointed out the large section of ruins they'd searched and said not to waste time there.

"Go on down a few hundred yards into that heavy timber," he advised, "and you'll find two dead horses. They've been shot and it looks like they fell off the cliff. I had just found them and came to tell Albert. I'm thinkin' the Chinese are up on the cliff and they killed those horses. Don't ask me why. You hombres figure it out. I've got to get to Durango!"

A mile or so away, Su Chang, having been assigned all the household duties, was cleaning dishes. After each meal she threw the leftovers out to land on a narrow ledge some fifteen or twenty yards below. She was fascinated to see that several bears had found their way to the food. After eating, they would disappear into the brush until the next day. She surmised that they must be coming up a steep, narrow trail hidden from view by the brush since they obviously weren't scaling the sheer face of the cliff.

One other thing got her attention that afternoon as she fed the bears. Six puffs of white smoke! *A signal*! *Someone is in the canyon!* Her pulse quickened as she stared into the distance. She glanced back to the cave to see if the others were watching. They were busy amusing themselves with a dice game.

They've seen nothin! she choked back her desire to cry for joy and walked back into the cave with an armload of clean dishes.

Later, she again stepped out into the sunlight-this time to dry some clothes she had washed in a pail of water. While her view of the trail in the canyon was partially obscured by heavy foliage, she did catch glimpses of a wagon moving on the trail to the ruins. She watched quietly, drying the clothing on sun baked rocks. Before returning to the cave, she saw the wagon driving out of the canyon. She wondered if someone was searching for her, and, if so, how she could signal to them. She remembered the mirror in her suitcase and decided she would start combing her hair outside in the sunshine.

Just before sun set on the western horizon, she excused herself and told Dao Chi that she would bring in the clothes that were drying outside.

When she didn't return in a short time, Dao Chi looked out to see that she was sitting on a rock combing her hair. He told her to get back into the cave. What he hadn't seen was that she had flashed several beams of light from her mirror to the canyon floor far below.

Meanwhile, the search was still going on.

"I'll go take a look at those horses," Malcolm said. "It shouldn't take but a few minutes."

Their condition left him just as puzzled as Hank. He looked

up the side of the cliff and couldn't see anything interesting but some caves which were inaccessible from the canyon. He walked back, and said, "I think I'll walk back down the trail for awhile. The cliffs there may have some clues. Those horses had to come from up there someplace."

"I'll come along," Angus said leaving Ted and Dutch to set up camp. "We should be back before dark."

They walked for a mile or more, scanning the cliffs, looking for any sign of human activity although they found it hard to imagine that anything other than animals would be inhabiting any of the caves.

As dusk approached they turned back toward camp.

Malcolm took one last glance.

"Wait!" he exclaimed. He put a hand on Angus' shoulder and pointed with his free hand.

"Look at that! It looked like a flash of light. See, around that large cave."

Angus looked and saw nothing but the cave.

"I don't see anything," he said.

"Well, I only saw one flash. It might have just been a reflection off a rock or a little waterfall. Anyway, the sun is behind the mountains now so we won't see it again today. Let's head back to camp," Malcolm replied, then said. "Look at those bears. See, there's two of them moving up the face of the cliff. I thought that would be way too steep for them to climb."

"Looks like they might have their own private trail," Angus answered, watching the two as they wove in and out of the dense foliage. "I'd say they are headed clear up to that cave if they can make it. Boy, they don't waste any time!"

"They're stopping short of the cave. Maybe they got where they're goin'. Can't tell from here. Well, it's going to be dark pretty quick. Guess we'd better forget the bears and head back," Malcolm said.

That night they all stayed in a large room that they found unique. It was completely round. The square and rectangular rooms throughout the ruins were all fairly small and may have been used as bedrooms, but the round rooms--and there were several of them--were usually large enough to hold many people. *Probably some sort of ceremonial rooms* was the consensus of opinion.

Again, the fear of maurading bears caused them to stand watch and no one slept well. They sat up late hoping that Albert made it back to Durango alive and trying to figure out where Su Chang the kidnappers had disappeared to. No wagon tracks had been located even though she had obviously entered the area in a wagon. The only clue was two dead horses lying at the bottom of a cliff.

"We walked along the rim earlier in our search and had to be close to where the horses went over the side. But we didn't see a thing," Malcolm said.

"Could you see into any of the caves that are close to the rim?" Dutch asked.

"Nope," answered Rolf. "Lookin' down you don't even see the caves. It's from down here lookin' up that you see 'em. I don't know how anyone would get down to one from the top. I'd be scared of the height. And it would take a mountain climber to get up from down here."

"You know," Malcolm chimed in, "I saw a bright light or reflection that looked like it came from one of the caves just before Angus and I came back. We must have been a mile from here. Didn't think a lot about it at the time but we may want to have another look. If someone was up there, flashing a mirror or a tin lid would be a good way to attract some attention."

CHAPTER 20

STEFFI AND THE TROUBLE AT ALEXANDER

When Steffi kissed Malcolm goodbye at the train station, her mind was already swimming with the things she had to do before he returned. First on her list would be to get their calves to auction the very next day. Malcolm told her that a new slaughterhouse was opening in Kansas City and buyers would be at the Alexander auction looking for heifers at about 800 pounds and steers at 1,000 pounds. Instinct told him that the market price would be high for 'finished' animals at those weights because of the severe drought the past two summers. Parched grass meant that most ranchers couldn't graze their animals in their pastures. Since little hay had been put up due to the lack of rain, the ranchers were forced to dispose of their herds over the past two years. Supply and demand meant that the shortage of cattle would push the price up.

While the drought was widespread, rainsqualls blowing in from Oklahoma territory had chosen a path across the Wandering S Ranch. It was a blessing. Two or three of those storms came just at the right time. Without that, their grass would have been gone, and, maybe the whole ranch.

Their heifers and steers, some 65 animals, had the necessary weights for the slaughterhouse buyers. They knew this was their best chance to dispose of the animals at a record profit. Failure to sell now meant the animals would get too large to attract the packing companies. The absence of those buyers would result in sizeable losses if the cattle had to be sold to cash starved ranchers.

Steffi knew she would need help to get the animals to the auction and she knew she could depend on Molly's husband, Jim.

It was already dark when she rode up to their sprawling ranch house. As she tied up her mare out front, she could see Molly and Jim through the kitchen window setting down to supper with their only son, little Pete--known as Petey Dinks--along with Colin and Hugh.

They had set an extra plate for her and were anxious for news from town. Steffi, between bites of roast beef with potatoes and gravy, brought them up to date on the investigation.

"Sounds like Malcolm and the rest of them might be gone for quite awhile. You've got some calves going to auction tomorrow. Why don't you stay here with the boys tonight?" Jim offered. "Molly can watch the kids tomorrow and we'll go over and start moving cattle. You'll need some help driving them to town."

"Thanks, Jim. It seems like we're always having to depend on you," Steffi replied, thankful for the offer. "But, we might even need some more people. Malcolm decided to sell off the fats since the new slaughterhouse in Kansas City is sending a buyer down. Is there anyone else we could get to help out on short notice? We've got about 90 head of fats to deal with in addition to the calves."

"I'll just head over and draft the Gresham twins. They owe me some work since I helped them raise their barn. Them boys got nothin' else to do anyway this time of year and it'll keep 'em out of trouble," Jim volunteered as he wiped his face and got up to leave.

"Can we get along with them?" Steffi asked, the tone of her voice reflecting her concern. "I hear they are getting tough to handle since they are growing up."

"'Dirty Bart' is the trouble maker but he don't really hurt anyone. He's just having fun. He got a snoot full a month or two ago down in Medicine and rode his mare into the Wild Horse Saloon. When they tried to throw him out, he shot off his six-shooter, blowing some holes in the ceiling. That little trick landed him in the pokey. 'Little Bert' tried to bust him out so the law threw him in too and they both wound up with seven nights free room and board. They calmed down a little and you don't see 'em around town much these days," Jim replied. "I'll go see if I can round them up for tomorrow. We'll all have to get up mighty early to make it to the auction on time."

Steffi and Jim were up riding long before dawn and arrived at the Wandering S just as the sun was bursting over the horizon.

Jim had seen the Gresham boys the night before and they agreed to help out. When they pulled up to the corral, the boys were already there "Raring to go!" 'Little Bert' said.

Steffi stole a sideways glance. *'Dirty Bart' certainly lives up to his nickname*, she thought looking at the greasy buckskins he was wearing, *but, 'Little Bert' looks a little cleaner*.

She was somewhat alarmed that each youth was carrying two six guns, a habit adopted by gunslingers who drifted through town but seldom seen on the 'locals'.

"They're just trying to look tough," Jim whispered to her after seeing the look on her face. "We can trust these boys, OK."

"All right," Steffi said, knowing that Jim could handle the boys. Her thoughts switched to the possibility of a couple of sick calves. She knew that if an epidemic spread among the herd, they would be ruined financially. She also knew the sale barn wouldn't accept sick cattle.

"Malcolm said a couple of head had dry noses," she said. Let's check 'em all before we start. We've got a big problem if any are going down on us."

Jim and the Gresham boys did a quick inspection, even rubbing the noses of some of the calves. Then, much to Steffi's relief, they announced that all the calves looked to be in good shape.

The calves were in the corral by the barn. Jim unlatched the gate and they started driving them down to the south pasture where the 'fats' were grazing.

The pasture was fenced on three sides. The backside didn't require fencing. It had a natural restraint provided by a rocky cliff that jutted up some two hundred feet into the air.

Jim swung the pasture gate open and they drove the calves in.

"Where do you suppose those crazy 'fats' think they are going," Steffi addressed the others as she saw the cattle they'd come for running in single file toward the base of the cliff. "That grass is grazed out and there's no water there."

"Hey! Look at that! Rustlers!" Dirty Bart yelled, his keen eyes picking out three men in the haze of the early dawn driving the cattle before them. "They are going to cut the fence down by the cliff and drive them out the back way!"

"Let's go after 'em," 'Little Bert' hollered as one of his six guns cleared leather. "There's only three. They ain't got a chance!"

"Yeehaaa! Let's go!" shrieked 'Dirty Bart, spurring his mount to a full gallop as he too jerked his pistol out of its' holster, anxious to show off his prowess as a gunman.

"Wait here with the calves!" Jim yelled at Steffi as he tore in behind the twins, pulling his carbine as he rode. "We'll run 'em off the property!"

Hearing the racket, Old Man Parcell and his two boys, Montie and Buddy saw they were in deep trouble.

This was their first attempt at a big time rustling job. They'd done well picking up a few strays along the way from Missouri, 'doctoring' the brands and selling them to marginal settlers who didn't care where they came from as long as they were cheap. Now it was obvious they were caught red handed and were going to have to run for it.

The old man sounded the alarm. "There's three of them coming for us. They left one at the main gate with another herd. We're up against a dead end if we hit the cliff and fence. If we break through, they'll run us down in the field beyond it. Here's what we do. When they get into shootin' range, we double back toward the entrance gate, keeping this herd between them and us. I don't think they'll shoot for fear of hitting the cattle. There's only one of them at the gate and we'll just gun him down. Then we'll drop down among those big boulders at the entrance and let the other three have it 'cause they'll be right on our tail. That's the only chance we've got! They're here! Let's go!" Old Man Parcell bellowed. They wheeled their horses, reversing their field and riding back toward the entrance at breakneck speed.

Jim and the Gresham twins, shocked by the rapid change of events, wheeled around in hot pursuit, enraged that they were outmaneuvered by the superb horsemanship of the rustlers.

"Ride!! Ride!!" Jim screamed at the top of his lungs knowing that Steffi was the only thing between the rustlers and the entrance gate.

Seeing that her life was now in jeopardy, Steffi weighed her options. She knew she couldn't outrun the rustlers nor could she make it back to the rocks in time to gain shelter.

Beside her was a fallen cottonwood tree. Knowing she was out of time, she grabbed her carbine from the scabbard, jacked a cartridge into the chamber, and fell on her stomach, using the trunk of the tree to steady her rifle. A vision of Malcolm and the boys appeared for a second and she prayed she would see them again.

The Parcells, on superior horses, were rapidly outdistancing Jim and the Greshams. In seconds they were within fifty yards of the cottonwood, firing in unison as they bore down on Steffi. Their shots slammed into the trunk, splintering bark and showering her with dirt and debris.

Calmly she fired her first round from about forty-five yards. Montie Parcell screamed and clutched his chest as the bullet tore into his breastbone. She worked the lever on the carbine again and heard another round slam home. She fired again, this time from about twenty-five yards. Buddy Parcell clawed at his throat as he tumbled from the saddle.

In a split second Old Man Parcell, riding at a full gallop, was upon her, spurring his horse in an effort to hurdle the cottonwood. At the top of his leap, the horses' left front leg caught in a branch and came tumbling down, throwing his rider into the dirt. There was no need for Steffi to load and fire again. Old Man Parcell was knocked cold.

Jim and the Greshams charged in and reined to a halt. 'Little Bert' then rode on and grabbed the reins of Montie Parcell's horse. Its rider had fallen dead from the saddle with one foot hooked in a stirrup. His head created a furrow in the soft dirt as the horse aimlessly drug him round and round in a tight circle.

Buddy Parcell laid dead on the ground, the shot that hit his throat allowed no time for suffering or repentance. They surmised that, he too, was dead when he hit the ground.

Old Man Parcell seemed to be coming around after his fall but his horse had broken its leg. 'Dirty Bart' put the animal down with one shot from his six-gun. "Ha!" he laughed, "that's the only shot I got off all day!"

"How you doing, Steffi?" Jim asked with obvious concern for his sister-in-law who had just been through an ordeal that would wreck most women for life.

She was sitting on the trunk of the cottonwood, nervously jacking shells out of the rifle, trying to calm her trembling body while she studied the faces of the men who had just tried to kill her.

"I can't believe all this happened. I'll bet it all didn't take two minutes. I haven't even had time to think about it. First I was there when Edna was killed, now I'm out here in the middle of all this. I don't know what to think about it."

As she spoke, Old Man Parcell, now awake, was helped to his feet by Jim.

"Could I have a shot of water?" he asked, favoring his right shoulder. Then said, rather apologetically, "I might have a busted collarbone."

"Sure," Jim said as he handed him his canteen. "Now maybe you can explain just what you and your gang thought you were trying to do."

"Ain't much to explain. These two are my sons. When they got out of the army--they'd both been in a Yankee prison--we went broke trying to farm in Missouri. We was starving to death so we decided to try our hand at rustling."

"Little lady," he said now turning his attention to Steffi, "you are a crack shot. But don't shed no tears over us. I told my boys we'd wind up at the end of a rope some day. You just saved them the agony."

Then he fell silent and stood looking at the ground, no longer appearing to be a bigger-than-life outlaw but just a little broken down old man whose life was now a shambles.

Jim turned to Steffi and the Gresham boys saying, "Steffi, I'll ride back and hitch up a buckboard. We'll have to haul these hombres into town with us. I'll be back in a few minutes."

When he returned, they loaded up the two bodies and Old Man Parcell. Steffi, now recovered enough to handle a team, took the reins while the men drove the cattle, trying to make up lost time and get to the auction before the sale started.

When they got to town, the cattle, which always have the right of way in ranch country, were driven down the main street and on to the corral, which was located next to the railroad yards.

Steffi stopped off at the little office of the town marshal where Nate Christopher was just unlocking the front door.

"Good grief, Steffi!" he stared at the cargo she was hauling. "What have you got here?"

She quickly filled him in on the details and said she'd be back with Jim and the Greshams to give him a complete statement as soon as the auction was over.

"Take your time, Steffi," Nate volunteered. "You've had a tough day already and I know you've got to take care of the cattle sale. I'll just lock this one up and go get Harold to haul the other two down to the mortuary. I'll be here whenever you get back."

A small crowd of curious onlookers, mostly people on their way to breakfast at the Goodnite Inn, were drawn by the sight of two corpses in the buckboard. They stood rubbernecking on the wooden sidewalk, taking in the conversation between Steffi and the lawman. Within minutes the story of Steffi's gunbattle and her bravery was sweeping the town.

News of her heroism had already reached the auction barn when she arrived. She was practically mobbed by the crowd who called for her to recount the story. They wanted a detailed blow-by-blow account of the action and Steffi could see there was no way the sale could start until she accommodated them.

"Come down here, Steffi, and tell us how you did it!" Big Jim Kincaid, the auctioneer called to her from his position in the sale ring. Everybody wants to know the story."

Somewhat reluctantly, Steffi entered the ring. Her entry was greeted by absolute silence as every cattleman and buyer there wanted to hear the whole thing.

"First of all, I'd like to say I wasn't alone. My brother-in-law, Jim Stevenson and the Gresham boys were with me then and I'd like for them to come down and join me here now."

She waved at the three who had just finished corralling the cattle so they sauntered down and stood next to her.

"I'm still a little nervous about the whole situation, she said with her voice cracking a bit, so I wonder, Jim, if you'd mind telling what happened out at our place this morning?"

Jim was an excellent talker. It took about ten minutes for him to describe the events of the day. He spared none of the details and his description of how Steffi virtually battled the three rustlers alone brought comments of awe from everyone in the barn.

Big Jim gave them another five minutes for questions and answers, then called out, "Well, now you've heard the story and there ain't a braver woman in the whole county. Let's get on with it and get her cattle sold! What do you say?"

Hats were tossed in the air as everyone whooped and hollered, their way of letting Steffi know how much they respected her and her bravery. Then, they each found a seat and the ring hands began driving in Steffi's cattle first, a courtesy to her as Big Jim could see she had other matters to attend to that day besides the cattle sale.

Prices bid went high. Then higher. The stocker calves went for fifty percent more than what Malcolm had predicted. Local ranchers were beginning to recover from the drought and their purchases showed it.

The fats had all survived the mad stampede and gun battle and were looking good to the packinghouse buyers from Kansas City. They were bidding against a Ponca City packer who also needed finished cattle for his operation.

Steffi wished Malcolm were there to see the unrestrained bidding between the two competitors. As the prices went beyond her wildest dreams, she realized that they would soon be entirely debt free and would have money in the bank. She made up her mind right then to pay off both their bank notes as soon as she had cash in hand.

The bidding finally ended with the Kansas City packer taking all the fats. But he paid dearly. Malcolm had been right about the shortage causing prices to go unreasonably high.

Steffi settled up with the auction clerk then asked Jim and the Greshams to meet her back at the marshal's office where they were to make their statements. She'd join them as soon as she made a quick stop at the bank.

Ben Wang was standing inside Chester's office when Steffi walked in. Seeing her, Chester waived her into his office. He and Ben were anxious to hear about her adventures that morning so she told the story again.

"Amazing, absolutely amazing!" Chester said. "Never thought you had it in you, Steffi! That took a lot of, if you'll excuse my language, guts."

Steffi just smiled and said, "Well, you just do what you have to. I didn't seem to have any other choices. Anyway, it's over and I've got to get over to Nate's office to make my statement. I thought I'd make this deposit here, Chester, before I do that. Also, I think we'll go ahead and pay off both our notes while we're at it."

"Have you got enough to cover all that?" Chester asked, then whistled as she handed him her check for the cattle proceeds.

"Yes, you certainly do!" he exclaimed, his eyes widening as he looked at the numbers. "I heard the cattle were going to go high, but I didn't think this high! I'll deposit this and pull your notes."

Chester stepped out to a cashier's cage, handed the check with some instructions to one of the girls, and returned. Steffi and Ben were discussing Malcolm and the search for Su Chang.

"Steffi, a telegram came this morning and Cletus brought it over here 'cause he heard you were going to be in town. It affects us all. It was sent from Durango by one of the deputies there. Here," Chester said, handing the paper to Steffi.

It read: PARTY SEARCHING MESA VERDE-STOP- NO SIGN YET-STOP-EVERYONE OK. It was signed by Hank Harrison, Deputy.

"Well, at least we know they got there and they're OK," Steffi, relieved to receive the news, responded, then inquired. "Isn't Mesa Verde an old Indian ruin outside of Durango?"

"It is," Ben answered. "We heard about it while we were in Colorado but we didn't have time to see it."

Looking at Ben's eyes, Steffi could see that he hadn't been getting any sleep. He looked completely exhausted. The worry over Su Changs kidnapping was taking its' toll.

"Ben," she said. "Try to get some rest. The people who have Su Chang have no reason to harm her. And I'll guarantee you one thing--Malcolm and Angus will never stop searching. They will bring her home to you!"

Ben appeared relieved at hearing these words of encouragement spoken so forcefully by the woman who'd shared Su Chang's terror during the kidnapping and murder at the Goodnite Inn.

"Steffi, we owe you and Malcolm a lot. Let me know how we can repay you," he said, tears brimming up in his eyes.

Steffi put her hand on his shoulder. "Don't give it a thought, Ben. You'd do the same for us and we know it! Well, I need to go for my boys and get a little rest myself. It's been a long day already," she said as her shoulders began to drop wearily.

"Just a second, Steffi," Chester caused her to pause at the

door. "Here's your deposit slip and your cancelled notes. Also, I know this isn't the time or the place to discuss it but I want to put a thought in your mind. The bank needs a new director to replace J. T. Ben and I think Malcolm would make a great addition to our group. Will you talk to him about it when he gets back?"

Steffi looked at Chester and thought, *Always the banker. He knows we've got some cash on hand now.*

"Sure, I'll talk to him. It might be a good thing," she replied as she left.

Outside, she almost bumped into J. T. Smith who was running up the bank steps with a telegram in his hands.

"Sorry Steffi," he said as he stepped back and tipped his hat. "Didn't see you comin'. I've got a message here that Chester is going to find interesting. Smooth Mouth Sam, the old prospector, and his boys just got gunned down at their mine in Arizona. This telegram was sent from Ft. Huachuca by Peg Leg Charlie. I outfit him at my store. He saw it all." She glanced at the telegram and he continued, "Also, congratulations are in order! I heard all about the fracas out at your place this morning. I can't believe you handled them hombres all by yourself."

"Maybe I was just lucky, J. T. Or, maybe a prayer was answered. Anyway, I don't ever want to have to try it again. It was really horrible. I was afraid I'd never see my family again. But, I certainly came out in better shape than these fellows. I didn't know them but I'm very sorry."

"Smooth Mouth was a fine old man, just trying to get away from prospecting and work the mine with his boys. Now this happens. It's tragic," J. T. replied. "Well, I better get inside. This news will interest Chester, I can tell you that. It was nice seein' you, Steffi."

Steffi rode on to the marshal's office.

She found Jim and the Gresham boys waiting so they all went in together to give their statements.

It only took about thirty minutes. When they got back

133

outside, Steffi offered to pay the boys for their work that day but they wouldn't take the money. "We owed Jim some time so we was glad to help," 'Little Bert' said.

"I appreciate that," Steffi said, "but I didn't expect to get you into a gun battle this morning. Here's a five dollar gold piece. You can split it. Just call it for 'hazardous duty'.

The Gresham boys, delighted with their newfound wealth, headed over to the town saloon to slake their thirst while Steffi and Jim climbed onto the buckboard to head back to his place.

Molly was holding supper for them. She'd heard about the gunfight from a cowboy out looking for strays. He'd stopped to water his horse and repeated the story he'd heard at the Goodnite Inn.

"You look all beat out, sis," Molly opened the door. Steffi started to answer but a sob caught in her throat. The women fell into each other's arms. Molly held her tight while Steffi bawled away the tensions of the day. In a few seconds, it was over. Steffi pulled away, mopping her eyes with her sleeve. "I'll be all right. I just had to get that out of my system. Where are the boys?"

"Out at the barn. They've eaten already. "While you're feeding your face you can fill me in on the details. A cowboy came by here today and said you are a genuine hero! I can't believe it! Are you really a gunfighter?"

Before she could answer, Colin and Hugh ran in shrieking and crawled up in her lap, followed by Petey Dinks who wanted a hug from his Aunt Steffi too.

It took a few minutes to get the boys settled down. By then, Jim had washed up so he joined them at the table while, between mouthfuls of cornbread and beans; Steffi related her story one more time.

After supper, Jim said, "I think I hear a rider," and stepped out on the porch. He was surprised to see 'Little Bert' come galloping in through the main gate on a heavily lathered mare.

"What's goin' on?" Jim asked as 'Little Bert' dismounted in a hurry, evidently with something urgent on his mind.

"Jim," 'Little Bert' began, "me and Bart was over to the saloon having a few beers when the three Calhoun boys and two of their scroungy friends come in. They'd been drinkin' some corn liquor and wasn't feelin' no pain. Anyway, they was all excited and talkin' about the rustlers. They'd heard that Steffi shot two of them and that Old Man Parcell was in jail. They was wantin' to have some fun so they got to agitatin' everyone in the bar and started talkin' about takin' the old man out of the jail to tar and feather him and ride him out of town on a rail. Lot of the boys thought that would be great fun. I told 'em I didn't like the idea but they told me to shut my mouth. I left Bart there to kind of keep an eye on things and I thought I'd better come out here and tell you and Steffi what's happening."

As 'Little Bert' spoke, Steffi and Molly, overhearing his comments, joined him and Jim on the porch.

"Nate ought to be able to handle a situation like that. He's the town marshal," Jim replied offering the logical solution.

"Problem is," 'Little Bert' continued, "that Nate is a cousin to the Calhoun boys. Nate don't have a lot of backbone and he even sat down and had a few drinks with the boys. If they get about four more down him he won't be in any condition to stop anyone. Also, there's probably twenty range cowboys or more come in on a trail ride from Texas this afternoon and they are all lookin' for some fun. It's gittin' pretty wild!"

Steffi interjected, "That old man may have tried to kill me but he's already paid a terrible price for that today. I know. I shot his two sons. There's no reason for him to have to be tortured and humiliated by a bunch of drunks. He'll stand trial for what he did. He may even have to swing for rustling, but that's for the court to decide."

Then she looked at 'Little Bert' and asked, "How far along have they got? What can we do about it?"

"Some of the boys had already gone to J. T.'s for a barrel of tar. They were building a fire in the street to heat it when I left. A couple more went over to Nelson's turkey farm to get some big feathers. I'd say in less than an hour they'll be ready. If we could get back there before they start, I think you could stop them," 'Little Bert' was looking straight at Steffi as he spoke. "Everyone in town says you are a hero. And, it's your cattle they was rustlin'. Looks to me like you are about the only one that can save the old man."

Steffi looked at Molly and shrugged her shoulders. "I'm tired enough to drop right here. Now we've got this situation. But I'm not going to let them hurt that old man!" Then she turned to Jim and asked, "Are you ready for another trip into town?"

Jim replied, "Sure, why not, but we'd better get crackin'. I just hope we can make it in time. I don't think that old man could stand a hot tarring as weak as he is."

Steffi looked at Molly and shook her head, saying, "Well, I hope you don't mind being stuck with the boys a little longer. We should be back in a couple of hours."

Molly hugged her and said, "You better move out. Times a wastin'."

Jim quickly saddled a horse for Steffi. Then he untied the mare that had been trailing the buckboard, mounted her and they galloped off, riding shoulder to shoulder with 'Little Bert' toward Alexander.

In town, the boys at the saloon were whooping it up in anticipation of the tar and feather party. The Calhoun boys had kept Nate Christopher's glass full all afternoon. Everybody knew the night marshal couldn't hold his liquor and they were all grinning as they watched him cradle his head in his arms as it slowly sank down to the table. Soon he was snoring loudly and it was a simple matter to lift the jailhouse keys from his pocket.

Outside the fire was roaring under a barrel of tar that was melting into a soft sludge. Soon it could be applied with a paintbrush.

The crowd spilled out of the saloon into the street, drunken cowboys firing their pistols in the air, laughing and staggering as they anticipated the good sport that awaited them, a sight that sent women, children, and the elder citizens of the town scurrying to their homes.

When two cowboys rode up with several flour sacks filled with feathers, cheers greeted them from the rabble who were now thirsting for action, goading each other on in their delirium.

In his cell across the street, Old Man Parcell cowered in terror. He'd seen the fire in the street heating the barrel of tar and watched the growing mob at the saloon. He was really worried because no one was guarding his cell. The night marshal was nowhere in sight. The old man knew he was doomed if the law didn't step in. He began to wish that Steffi had finished him off with his two boys. Being tarred caused skin to stop breathing. If someone cleaned a tarred victim up quickly with kerosene, he had a chance of living. If not, death would come in an agonizing fashion.

Then they came for him. It was a rush of humanity that unlocked his cell, and oblivious to his cries for mercy, passed him like a sack of flour over their heads, one man to another until he was deposited unceremoniously face down in the dirt in front of the blazing tar barrel.

As he rose up on one knee to get to his feet, a heavy boot crashed into his face causing him to stagger and fall on his back.

"Tie him!" Then get some tar on them brushes! We're going to have a party!" Joe Calhoun shouted with glee, a cry abruptly changing to a curse as he leaped sideways and danced in the dust to avoid three pistol shots that boomed out, aimed straight at his toes.

He went for his six gun as he faced his tormenter but thought better of it as he was staring down the barrel of 'Little Bert's' .44.

"Are you out of your skull? You like to killed me!" he shouted at the gunman. "I ought to have you horsewhipped!"

"Get back and shut up!" 'Little Bert' ordered, his pistol still aimed at Calhoun's head. "Steffi here wants to say something to all of you."

The crowd parted and calmed down a bit as Steffi and Jim walked their horses into the center of the mob.

Old Man Parcell, greatly relieved to see them--an irony since he would have killed them both earlier in the day if he could-- staggered to his feet and stood between their two horses.

"You boys are all out here to have a good time," Steffi began. "But you are just about to the point of committing murder! If you think you are doing me a favor by tarring and feathering this old man, you are sadly mistaken! I don't want any part of it and you'd better not! You probably don't know that hot tar can kill a man in a fairly short period of time. This man hasn't even been tried yet and already you are ready to torture him to death! And remember, murder is punishable by hanging! All of you out there that are willing to hang for murder, just raise your hand right now!"

For a moment or two dead silence greeted her offer and nobody raised a hand. Firm in her position she continued to sit erect in her saddle her gaze shifting directly into the eyes of the Calhoun boys, the obvious ringleaders.

The cowboys and other thrill seekers looked at each other kind of sheepish, realizing that a woman was putting them down.

Then Cleve Calhoun spoke up, his nerves shaken by the direct eye contact coming from Steffi. "Ain't nobody lookin' to kill anyone, Steffi. I guess we all got a little likkered up and thought we'd teach the old rustler a lesson. Thought we was doin' you a favor but I guess you don't see it that way."

"Now you're talkin'," Steffi replied. Then, raising her voice, cried out. "This party is over boys! Everybody move out!"

Without a word, the mob turned on their heels as one, heeding her command as though they were soldiers on parade.

"Here's the keys to the jail," Joe Calhoun said, handing them to Jim. "Nate is so drunk he can't do nothin' so I guess you can play jailer for awhile."

"God bless you," Old Man Parcell said as Jim and Steffi locked him back in his cell. "About two minutes more and I was a goner. Them boys was serious about slapping that hot tar to me!"

"Well, I don't know if your life is going to get any easier from here on out, but at least you shouldn't have any more trouble from that bunch. They just got carried away on corn liquor," Steffi said as she and Jim turned their horses back toward the ranch.

Ben Wang, crouched behind an open window in his apartment, viewed the entire event through the sights of his Winchester trained on the chest of Joe Calhoun.

There is no woman braver than Steffi Frazier, he thought as the crowd dispersed. *And her husband is out trying to rescue my wife. Nobody has ever helped us more. I need to talk to her and Malcolm about the bank directorship. They have no idea of the opportunity awaiting us all.*

Lying on his bed were some papers he'd been reviewing. Papers that could spell major changes in the lives of many people. One was the old newspaper article about the planned Transatlantic Cable and the shortage of copper. He also had a copy of his purchase of bank stock which made him the major stockholder. A third document was a copy of the assignment of Smooth Mouth Sam's mine stock to J. T. Smith. Then last, but certainly not least, a subsequent transaction whereby J. T. signed his rights in that mining stock over to the bank.

He scanned the documents again to see if he could detect any legal flaws or errors in them. Satisfied there were none he opened his dresser drawer and put them in with some other items of importance.

He pulled another piece of paper out that he'd gotten from Chester and glanced at it. It was the telegram from Peg Leg Charlie telling of the murder of Smooth Mouth and his boys at the mine.

Ernest C. Frazier

CHAPTER 21

STRANGE COMMUNICATIONS

Sleep came slowly for Malcolm that night. He kept thinking about the light he'd seen flashing the night before, a possible signal from Su Chang. At dawn he announced that he was going back to investigate. Angus again volunteered to go along. Rolf, who wanted no part of the heights at all, said he'd keep searching the canyon. Dutch and Ted agreed to stay and help him. Maybe they could solve the mystery of the dead horses.

Two hours later, Su Chang, hairbrush and mirror in hand, and Dao Chi were at the mouth of the cave catching a breath of air.

"Look down," Dao Chi ordered, wiping the fog off his spectacles. "Did something move down in the canyon?"

Su Chang looked and saw what appeared to be two men moving into the brush. Glancing at Dao Chi she saw he still had his glasses off and was depending on her sight.

"May have been bears," she said. "Sometimes they get into the berry bushes in the morning. They are out of sight now."

Dao Chi put his glasses back on and continued to stare down. He saw nothing moving and decided to go back inside.

"I'll finish my hair and will come back in a minute," Su Chang said from her rock perch.

Once Dao Chi was out of sight, she began flashing her mirror again and again in an attempt to attract attention from below. After a few seconds she returned to the cave.

Her efforts were not in vain. "Angus, look!" Malcolm exclaimed from his spot on the trail. "Lights flashing!"

"Yeah, I see. Someone wants to get our attention. But we got a problem," Angus replied, looking at the cliff's sheer face.

"Well, let's take a look for the trail the bears were using last night. It looked like they've got a path, at least as far as that ledge," Malcolm was already moving into the brush as he spoke.

It didn't take long in the sunlight to discover their route. It followed a natural outcropping of rocks and bushes and made a gradual ascent, traversing across the face of the cliff until it ultimately arrived at the ledge below the cave. The natural cover would conceal any climber.

"I think we've found a way to get up to the ledge," Malcolm said. "But when we get there, it looks like it's still another ten or twenty yards--it's hard to tell from here--to the mouth of the cave. Even if we got up there and found Su Chang, the Tong would spot us and pick us off. If we got a rope and came down from the top, they would hear us before we ever made it."

"We need to be able to communicate with her, but I don't see how that's possible," Angus responded as he studied the situation.

"I don't know," Malcolm, equally puzzled, answered. "Maybe we'll think of something tonight. In any event, I think we found 'em and I'll give those Chinese credit. They really know how to hide out where nobody would look. Our problem will be figuring out how to get her out without gettin' us all killed. Let's head back. Maybe the others will have some ideas."

They made it about half way back to camp when gunshots rang out, sending them diving into the brush for cover. Two rapid shots from a .44 followed by a third a moment later boomed through the canyon--fired from the direction they were headed!

"The boys must be in bad trouble! I don't know if they're shootin' at someone or if they are being shot at but we'd better make tracks and get our fanny's back there quick! They'd never fire a gun around here unless it's serious!" Malcolm exclaimed as he and Angus doubled their pace to a steady trot.

Bad trouble was right! While Rolf was searching the ruins, Dutch and Ted had walked down to examine the dead horses lying in the timber. They hadn't counted on a rogue bear, drawn by the smell of horsemeat, scouring the area at the same time. Ted had recoiled instinctively, falling backward as he almost collided with the animal--a starving brute with only one paw. Snorting with rage at the intrusion into his territory, the bear charged. But Dutch was lightning quick. He yanked his .44 from its' holster, firing two rounds point blank into the bear's head who was rolling Ted in the dirt with his one good paw. Before Dutch could get off his third round the animal wheeled and flattened him with a pulverizing blow. The .44 sounded one more time as Dutch fired from flat on his back, another head shot that finished the bear for good.

Rolf arrived seconds later and assessed the damage. Both men could walk even though they had gaping wounds to their arms and shoulders. Rolf pulled off his shirt and tore it into strips which he used as bandages. Back at camp, he found a bottle of whiskey in the medicine chest. Ignoring their protests, he seared their bodies as they writhed in pain.

"I'm going to have to take both of you back to town," he said. "No need to argue. If you get blood poisoning there's no way we can save you out here in the mountains. Let's mount up. I'll ride along 'cause both of you are lookin' mighty pale. We'll meet Malcolm and Angus on the trail and tell 'em what happened. They won't like the gunfire but there wasn't any other choice."

When they met a few minutes later, Malcolm and Angus agreed that they had to fire on the rampaging bear.

Malcolm told them about the signals from the cave and that he believed they had been flashed by Su Chang.

"Let's hope so!" Rolf exclaimed, delighted that the search could end soon. "I wish I could be with you to flush 'em out, but I've got to stay with these boys. I don't know if they can hold out with the amount of blood they lost. 'Course, if there's any mountain climbing to be done, I just can't handle it so I might as well be the one to leave. Only thing is, I don't have any idea how you're going to scale that cliff, either from the top or bottom without being seen."

"Rolf, you boys may have just solved our problem. You go on back to town and we'll take care of the situation here. Don't worry about us. Angus and I can handle it from here on in," Malcolm said, looking at Rolf for approval.

"How do you propose to do that?" Rolf asked. "They may have you outgunned and we don't want Su Chang hurt in any way."

"I'm just now figuring out my plan. We're going to try to get up to a ledge just beneath the cliff and establish communication with Su Chang. We'll take care to see to it that neither she nor us gets hurt. I'll back off the plan if it looks too dangerous. I promise," Malcolm said.

"Well, I'll trust in your good judgment. Just don't let us down," Rolf replied as he and his two wounded companions began their slow ride back to town.

"What've you got on your mind, Malcolm? What're you thinkin'?" Angus asked.

"This may sound dumb, but here's my idea," Malcolm began. "First of all, let's remember that every day it looks like several bears go up to that ledge beneath the cave. I suppose Su Chang or somebody else is throwing them table scraps. Now, it's obvious that a man can't get up to that ledge without drawing attention to himself. But a bear can."

"Malcolm, we can't train a bear to go up there and do anything for us," Angus responded, looking at Malcolm with wonder.

"You're right. But--and here's the hard part to believe--a man dressed in a bearskin could make it up there, couldn't he?" Malcolm asked.

Angus grinned and chuckled as he grasped the idea. "Now you are makin' sense. And, by coincidence, we just happen to have a bear right here ready to be skinned!"

"That's it," Malcolm replied. "It sounds incredible but I don't know of any other way to sneak up to that cave. So, I'll go up there dressed in a bearskin. People looking down from above should think I'm the real thing. Hopefully Su Chang will come out of the cave. If the sun's out, I can flash her some signals off a tin lid. She's smart enough to know it's not a bear doing it. She'll figure out how to get a message to me. Then, we'll just have to see what happens. What do you think about that for a far fetched, screwball idea, but one that just might work?"

"Well, I don't know of any other way to get a man up there. I suppose I'll have to tail along and cover you from the bushes with my Winchester. If they discover you, you're a sittin' duck perched out on that ledge, lookin' like a fool in a bearskin," Angus grinned as he was getting into the feel of the plan.

"You've got it figured. Now we've got a skinnin' job to do. That might take all night so let's get started!" Malcolm pulled his giant bowie knife from his boot.

The next morning Su Chang followed her ritual of pitching out the table scraps. Usually there were three or four bears on the ledge. Today there was only one in sight as she discarded some hard tack and beans, aiming for the ledge below. A reflection caught her eyes as she dumped the pail. She glanced toward the source and another flash crossed her vision. *That bear can't be flashing signals!* she thought. Then her heart began pounding with the realization that she was looking at a man disguised as a bear!

He elation was short lived. It was replaced by quiet panic when Dao Chi walked out to join her. "I see only one bear came today," he said as he pitched a piece of biscuit downward. "Where are the others?"

"I don't know," Su Chang replied, practically holding her breath as the 'bear' picked up a biscuit and devoured it. "He is the only one that I saw."

Dao Chi, watched with idle curiosity for a while then observed, "That old bear only has one paw. He can't hunt so that's why he's reduced to begging for food. If he figures a way to do it, he'll try to get up to our cave. He can smell our food. I will kill him."

He drew his .44 and took careful aim. Su Chang stood in

mute terror as she saw his thumb whiten with the strain of drawing the hammer back. He stood as steady as a rock for a few seconds. She finally allowed herself to breathe when he lowered the pistol and said, "I should kill him right now but a gunshot would draw attention. But if he gets up here, I will have no choice."

He stayed a few more minutes scanning the canyon floor. Detecting nothing out of the ordinary and bored with bears and small talk, he turned to back to the cave and said, "Don't stay out here very long. I heard something like gunshots yesterday. There may be hunters around here."

Once she regained her composure, Su Chang acknowledged the signals by flashing her mirror several times at the 'bear' below. She then quickly walked back into the cave.

"It's such a beautiful morning. I think I will sketch the mountains," she said to the others. She picked up some rough paper, a pencil and a bit of charcoal left over from the nightly fire.

Her companions had already begun their daily game of dice, their only diversion from the monotony of cave dwelling, and paid scant attention as she left.

Good, she thought as she saw the 'bear' waiting below. *He is still there.*

She sat down and wrote a brief message: I AM SU CHANG. 3 MEN HOLD ME CAPTIVE. I HAVE ROPE LADDER AND CHLOROFORM. COME AT MIDNIGHT. THEY WILL NOT WAKE UP. Then she took an empty bully beef tin, stuck the note into it and let it roll down the face of the cliff where the 'bear' picked it up, read it, waived to her and quickly disappeared from the ledge into the bushes.

CHAPTER 22

HIGH MOUNTAIN RESCUE

"Getting up a rope ladder at midnight is goin' to be one tough job. It looks like a good fifteen or twenty feet from the ledge up to the cave," Angus observed. "Not only that, but look outside. It's startin' to drizzle. Sure we don't want to call this off until tomorrow night?"

"Nope," Malcolm answered. "I wouldn't be surprised if they try to move as soon as the weather clears up. They had to be spooked when our boys shot the bear and I don't think they are goin' to stick around. If we don't get her tonight, we may not get another chance."

"Well, it's your funeral. You said you could handle a rope ladder. How well can you climb when it's pitch black and raining?" Angus asked. "I doubt if there will be a moon tonight."

"Look, it's all done by feel," Malcolm explained. "I just have to go up one rung at a time. My main concern is the length of the ladder. I'd guess they came down by ladder from the top of the rim to the cave. From what we saw, that's about the same distance as from the ledge up to the entrance. If that's right, probably the ladder Su Chang's goin' to throw to us is long enough. If it's too short, I'll never make it."

"If she chloroforms them kidnappers then can't get the ladder to us, she'll have a big set of problems when they wake up," Angus expressed his fears while searching his mind to come up with an alternate plan.

"We're just goin' to have to bet on the ladder doin' the job. That's all we can do. We'd better start now. It'll be pushing midnight before we get to the ledge," Malcolm strapped on his .44 as he spoke.

147

Su Chang struggled for control as panic threatened to send her body into violent spasms. That afternoon she overheard Dao Chi say they were going to leave at sunrise and find another remote spot. He was worried about the gunshots from the canyon and believed they were in danger.

She believed her rescuers would come at midnight, a mission she couldn't delay regardless of the growing storm. The rain was falling in a steady drizzle, creating a terrible hazard. To complicate matters, the chloroform would have to be administered as her captors slept, an act requiring raw courage and calm hands. There was no room for failure. If she faltered, they would awaken. She dreaded to consider her fate if that occurred.

As the hours dragged on, she tossed on her blanket, listening to the rhythmic snoring in the next room. Flashes of lightning provided enough light for her make out the hands on her pocket watch. As midnight approached, she took a series of deep breaths to choke down her fear, then rose silently, and on palsied legs slipped into the adjoining room.

It was quite dark but she had committed the room and everything in it to memory. She dropped to her knees and groped around for the chloroform bottle, freezing momentarily as Dao Chi rolled in his sleep. Finally she located the bottle. She paused and hugged herself as hard as she could for a good two minutes to control her shaking, then gathered the strength to unscrew the cap. But her spirits sunk and she had an insane desire to scream when she saw that the bottle was nearly empty! Realizing she had to press on, she soaked her handkerchief with the remaining liquid and slowly brought it to the open mouth of Dao Chi, praying that there was enough solution to incapacitate him. She had nothing to fear. His breathing merely deepened as the drug took hold. She repeated the performance, using the same handkerchief on the two coolies with the same results.

After removing their weapons, she moved to the entrance where her hands found the heavy rope ladder piled on the floor.

She deposited the pistols in some brush and picked up the ladder.

Staggering under the burden, she drug it to the edge of the cliff. From below she heard three sharp whistles, sounds that caused her to sob with relief at the knowledge that her rescuers were there. Working quickly, her movements being illuminated by repeated flashes of lightning across the blackened sky, she secured the top rung of ropes to the base of a gnarled scrub pine.

Patches of moonlight filtered through the storm clouds. Combined with the lightning, they illuminated the ledge below. As she lowered the ladder over the edge she could make out the forms of two men waiting.

Then she heard a faint voice calling up to her. It was Malcolm, saying, "Su Chang, the ladder won't reach us. Can you move it five or six feet closer?"

Several jagged rocks protruded from the face of the cliff. They provided the ideal spot to anchor the rope.

But it wasn't an easy task.

Time and again she fell on the slippery incline at the cliff's edge as struggled with the rain soaked ladder. Each time she grabbed onto the thorny bushes to keep from being swept over the side. Besides having to contend with the ladder, the icy rain, and bleeding hands, her horrible fear of heights made her feel that she was moving in slow motion.

It was a monumental task for a one hundred and ten pound woman. She could feel her strength waning. It was taking much too long and she didn't know how long she could depend on the chloroform. Her captors could awaken at any time!

She finally got a loop over a rock and staggered back to catch her breath. A mighty tug from below tested her work.

"Cover me," Malcolm said. "I'm going up. It's secured."

While Angus held the rope taut, Malcolm moved up the sheer face of the cliff, pausing as lightning, thunder and rain threatened to drive him back to the safety of the ledge. Ignoring it all, he doggedly continued upward. It only took a few minutes, and then he was at the top, reaching to grasp Su Chang's outstretched hand.

Then, he was next to her, holding her as she hugged him, gasping for air to regain his strength.

"We made it! We're going to get you out of here right now! Are all three men in the cave?" he asked, whispering excitedly to her.

"Yes. I used the chloroform but the bottle was almost empty. They may wake up at any time! We must hurry!" she warned.

Then she screamed, a hysterical shriek that even Angus could hear over the sounds of the storm.

Standing in the entrance to the cave, groggy from the effects of the drug, stood Dao Chi and the two coolies, taking deep gulps of air to clear their heads.

"Quick, down the ladder!" Malcolm barked at Su Chang. "It's your only chance!"

Su Chang screamed again as one of the coolies, having gathered his senses leaped forward and struck Malcolm from behind, delivering a savage knee kick to the kidneys.

Rolling to the side to avoid another blow, Malcolm drew and fired one round from his .44 into the man's chest, dropping him without a whimper.

Then the other two were on him. Dao Chi kicked the pistol from his hands as his companion delivered a crunching blow to the face.

Dropping the rope, Su Chang leaped on the back of the coolie in an attempt to save her rescuer as he battled Dao Chi at the cliffs' edge for possession of his pistol.

"Kill her!" Dao Chi shrieked as he tripped, pulling Malcolm down with him in the mud. "Throw her off the cliff!"

From below, Angus, his view illuminated by the electrical storm, was helpless as the scene unfolded.

While his Winchester was at his shoulder, he couldn't risk firing even as the coolie, whirling like a dervish, wrenched Su Chang from his back.

She clawed and fought like a madwoman, but was no match against the powerful coolie.

Malcolm broke free and tried to reach her, only to be tackled and drug down again by Dao Chi.

Still unable to get a shot off, Angus could do nothing as Su Chang, her hand locked in a death grip on the coolie's shirt collar, was raised high in the air then hurled over the face of the cliff!

Angus leaped into position as she hurtled toward the ledge, followed by the screaming coolie who'd been jerked off balance by his victim.

Angus braced himself, staggering as he absorbed the complete shock of her body slamming into his. The force of her weight flattened him, stunning him as they crashed to the ground. Her body bounced from the impact and she almost slid over the edge. But one powerful hand hung on, pulling her back to safety.

"Are you all right?" Angus asked as they lurched to their feet.

"Yes!" she gasped. "I can't believe you caught me. You could have been killed!"

"Don't worry about me. Look up there!" he shouted.

They watched as the two combatants, standing upright, wrestled for position. Malcolm flattened Dao Chi with a clubbing right hand to the temple. He leaped to press his advantage only to be met by an explosive kick to the face delivered by his acrobatic adversary who sprang from his back with his feet flying. Again, Malcolm fell under the onslaught. The moonlight caught the reflection of a dagger as Dao Chi pulled it from his boot. He held the weapon's handle with both hands, preparing to drive it to the hilt.

Angus' Winchester boomed once. Dao Chi appeared to be suspended between heaven and earth as his body, shocked by the impact of the slug, jerked uncontrollably for a minute. Then, life left him. He slumped forward and slowly slid over the precipice. Angus and Su Chang jumped back as his body hit the ledge then careened off into space, joining his comrade in the valley below.

"Are both of you OK?" Malcolm shouted as he caught his breath.

"No problem. Su Chang is all right. Do you want me to come up?" Angus called back.

"No. All we've got up here is one dead man. I'll tie a lasso on his feet and let him over the side. We'll take him back with us. Ask Su Chang if I can bring her anything from the cave," Malcolm called out.

"Everything I have is in that suitcase in the back!" she shouted back. "That's all I need."

Shortly thereafter, the body of the dead coolie came sliding down to the ledge, followed by the suitcase.

Malcolm arrived moments later, bleeding from the nose and mouth. He'd taken a savage beating at the hands of Dao Chi.

"Are you all right?" Su Chang asked while embracing him with gratitude.

"I'll be all right," Malcolm responded. "I may have a broken nose. And I can't see out of my left eye. The important thing is that you're not hurt."

"Angus is a strong man. He broke my fall. I thank you both! Without you, I would be a captive of the Tong for the rest of my life," Su Chang examined his face as she spoke, then added, "Your eye is swelling shut."

"I think it's just a black eye. It'll be fine," Malcolm said. "But we got you and that's what we came for. Now, we'll get you back home to Ben. He's worried sick. He wanted to come along but the sheriff asked him to stay away. Too much danger for the two of you to be out here at the same time. We'd better move on now. The storm is breaking up."

The rain had stopped, a blessing as the clouds drifted away allowing the moonlight to illuminate the trail.

"We'll stay in the ancient village tonight. Tomorrow we'll round up the other two bodies and head back to Durango," Malcolm said as they began the slow descent back into the canyon.

Ernest C. Frazier

CHAPTER 23

PEG LEG CHARLIE

Peg Leg Charlie left the Provost Marshal's office at Ft. Huachuca scratching his head.   He'd just experienced the Government bureaucracy first hand and he couldn't deal with it. First of all, he'd reported the killings at the mine and was advised that it wasn't a military matter. He'd have to advise the sheriff in Tombstone, or the U. S. Marshal in Tucson.

"Can we send telegrams from here?" he'd asked.

He'd been directed to the telegrapher in an adjoining room where he sent his first wire to J. T. Smith advising him of the shootings at the mine.   Then he wired the sheriff's office in Tombstone. A response came in a few minutes. The telegrapher read it to Peg Leg: "SHERIFF WOUNDED IN HOSPITAL-STOP-NO HELP AVAILABLE-STOP. A clerk had signed it.

"Let's try Tucson.   There's got to be a marshal there," Peg Leg said.

They'd waited two hours for a response to their wire. When it came, Peg Leg knew he'd been wasting his time. It read: ALL U. S. MARSHALS AT FLORENCE PRISON RIOT-STOP. It too was signed by a clerk.

"Dad burn it!" the old prospector cried out in disgust, slapping his pants with his hat. "I'll get some help out at that mine even if I have to go back to Kansas. People out there I know will be glad to help a fellow out!"

Not knowing exactly what to do, he began riding back toward the mine, drawn there by the thoughts of Smooth Mouth and the boys. He thought, *if those gunslingers got back from Tombstone, they'll have buried the bodies. If they didn't, I will. I won't have 'em laying out there rottin'.*

Two days later he was within a half mile from the mine.

Once again caution told him to hobble and muffle his animals and approach on foot.

He was well concealed by a shallow arroyo that ran by the mine. Twenty yards from the entrance, he peered over the top. *Good!* he thought, seeing three freshly covered graves. *The boys have been buried proper.*

His attention was diverted to the sounds of a hammer driving nails. The two killers, Bob and Sy, had painted two large signs with red paint. They were nailing them onto poles a couple of hundred yards away where the main road forked to the mine. Peg Leg could read one of them. It read: DANGER! ABANDONED MINE CAVE IN! DO NOT APPROACH! DANGER!

Their plan was apparent to him. No one in his right mind would enter a mining area with those warnings posted. *Them claim jumpers are pretty smart. Ain't nobody goin' to get close to them so they can dig in peace. I wonder what Smooth Mouth and his boys found that was worth gettin' killed fer? I might jist have to do a little snoopin' around here.*

For five days, he watched from the arroyo as the killers turned miners brought up load after load of ore. On the sixth day, they strapped water barrels on their horses and rode away to the east, evidently for fresh water. That provided Peg Leg with the chance to examine the ore. He studied it with his prospector's eye. *Copper, they've hit copper.*

Taking a greater risk, he lit a lantern and entered the mine. He hadn't gone in twenty yards until he could see the rich vein reflecting off the light.

Tons and tons of it, he thought as he penetrated deeper into the shaft, tracing the vein with his finger, marveling at the quantity and quality of the high-grade ore. *Must be the biggest vein in the country. They must think there's a market for it.*

He was puzzled. Most miners he knew only went for gold and silver. He knew of no major market for copper.

Putting out the lantern, he cautiously retraced his steps to the entrance. Seeing no one, he slipped back to the arroyo, following it back to the donkeys where he had his camp.

When it was dark, he went back to the mine to see if the two killers had returned. Their horses were hobbled and four barrels of fresh water stood nearby. A light shone from the shack they used as a home.

Peg Leg crept up to the window. He saw they were getting ready for bed. There was a crawl space under the cabin. Risking an encounter with a snake or a scorpion, he gingerly crawled into the area until he was underneath them. From there he could hear them talking.

"Partner, this mining ain't near as much fun as I thought it'd be. How many tons do we have to dig 'fore we call for someone to haul it to the smelter?" Bob asked.

"I don't know. We may be diggin' for 30 to 60 days. Jist depends on how long it takes to get enough to fool with. Maybe we'd ought to hire some help. I'm wearin' out myself. I ain't used to havin' blisters on my hands," was the reply.

Bob continued, "I don't know who we could trust. I guess if someone comes along lookin' fer work we can check 'im out. We need help, that's fer shore. We can explain the graves by sayin' they was here when we bought the mine. Another thing, do you reckon old Jed really knows what he's talkin' about? He said this copper is goin' to be worth a fortune when the gov'ment starts buyin' it."

"If it ain't worth a bunch, we're going to look mighty stupid. But that newspaper article about a copper cable going clear to London looked pretty good to me. We might be millionaires already and don't even know it!" Sy exclaimed, reassuring Bob of their wise decision. "Maybe we'd better get a little sleep. Sun rises early out here. Hey! What was that? Did you hear a bumping sound?"

Peg Leg held his breath. A tarantula creeping on his neck had caused him to jerk his head forward, banging it on a floor joist.

"Aw, that's jist an old pack rat. They're all over the place," Bob answered.

"Maybe so, but I'm goin' out to have a look around," Sy picked up his .44 as he rolled out of bed and headed for the door. "I'll be back in a minute."

Peg Leg, laying flat on his back, pulled his revolver from its' holster. Sand poured from the barrel. Immobilized by fear, he knew the gun could misfire or explode in his face if he squeezed off a round.

Sy walked out of the shack and circled it a couple of times. Peg Leg almost jumped out of his skin as Sy's pistol fired one time, splitting the night air. He relaxed a little when he heard Sy shout, "Hey Bob, jist got me a nice fat skunk! He was over at the woodpile!"

"Man that thing stinks!" Bob hollered back. "Did'ja have to shoot 'im right here?"

"Yeah, he was headed fer the shack. Probably hides there all the time. He was about to make a clean getaway," Sy answered as he walked back into the building.

Peg Leg continued to laid quietly for another hour or so, nauseated almost to the point of vomiting by the noxious odor. Finally, he could hear heavy snoring so he slid out from the crawl space and headed back to camp.

Dawn saw him riding away toward Tombstone. He knew from there he could make the necessary connections by stagecoach and rail to get him up to Kansas. He had some information he wanted to share with his friends in Alexander.

CHAPTER 24

CELEBRATION

Cletus Morgan tore out of the depot, raced up the street to the Goodnite Inn and slapped the wire from Malcolm down on Ben's table where he was having morning tea. "Look at this! They've got Su Chang and they're comin' home!" Cletus, normally quite reserved, startled Ben with his uncharacteristic outburst.

Ben scanned the message. He noticed everyone in the dining room staring at him. Knowing they were as thirsty for a report as himself, he rose and shared the good news, "They'll be home on the train tomorrow! Su Chang is safe. Malcolm and Angus have rescued her and they are all coming back!"

Then he turned to Raymond Crocker and said, "Raymond, here's a silver dollar. Will you go to Binfords and have him saddle my black gelding? Then ride out and tell Steffi the news. Here, take this so she can read it herself. She'll want to be here when the train comes in tomorrow."

In a flash the boy was out the door and on his way.

An hour later Steffi was hanging up clothes while the boys played in a sand pile. The sound of the gelding's hooves beating a tattoo on the hard packed road announced Raymond's arrival. Riding for all he was worth, the lad reined up and yelled, "Guess what? Malcolm is coming home! Him and Angus saved Su Chang!"

He leaned from his saddle and offered her Malcolm's telegram.

Steffi snatched the paper and read the message several times. When Raymond dismounted to water his horse, she grabbed and hugged him, taking him somewhat aback as she began to cry, "Thank you, thank you, thank you! You don't

159

know how happy you've made me!" Then, composing herself and considering the situation at hand, she wiped her eyes and continued, "We're having a late breakfast. Could you stand some bacon and eggs?"

"Sure could," Raymond, never one to turn down home cooking, replied. He tied the horse and followed her and the boys into the house.

During their meal Steffi asked him a question he thought was a little odd. She asked if he knew who his parents were and if he knew their whereabouts. He told her he new nothing of them as he was abandoned at birth and had lived on a 'poor farm' until he was old enough to strike out on his own.

She didn't pursue her question further, letting the subject drop as she began cleaning up after the meal.

"If you'll wait a few minutes I'll harness up Old Dolly to the buckboard and the boys and I'll ride into town with you. I really want to talk to Ben. He's got to be excited!" Steffi said, too agitated to stay around the house any longer.

"Sure, in fact I can harness her up while you finish the dishes," Raymond replied, always anxious to be of help.

Soon they were on the trail, making one brief stop where Steffi told Molly the news.

"Look," Molly said, "leave the boys here. The train comes in tomorrow. You might as well stay in town tonight and save runnin' back and forth. Knowing Ben, he'll plan a big blowout at the restaurant to welcome 'em back and you can't miss that! Jim'll watch your livestock, so you go ahead and have a good time!"

"Well, you know me. My suitcase is always packed. I'll just take you up on that deal! But, we'll expect you to be our guests for Sunday dinner at the hotel. Agreed?"

Molly, needing a little socializing of her own, nodded her head as she saw Steffi and Raymond on their way.

When they got to town, Raymond stopped at Binfords to rub down the gelding while Steffi continued on to the Goodnite Inn. It was lunchtime and she could see a larger-than-usual crowd was gathered in the dining room with the overflow standing in the foyer.

Ben waved at her from his table that was already crowded with well-wishers, and called for a waitress to bring another chair.

"Greetings, Steffi," Ben, always the gracious host said as he seated her. "I suppose Raymond delivered the telegram to you?"

"Ben, that's the greatest news I ever received in my life and I know you feel the same way!" Steffi replied. "I'm amazed at how quickly they found her!"

"Malcolm and Angus must be good detectives. I'm very anxious to hear their story. The telegram didn't tell us very much and everybody in town wants to talk to them. Steffi, here's what I want to do, and I'm asking you to be a part of it. I'd like to decorate the dining room with 'welcome home' banners and host a large buffet tomorrow night featuring barbequed beef for anyone who wants to come. Then we'll have a dance afterward. I'll pay for it all since it was my Su Chang who was rescued. This is my way of celebrating. I can even supply some Chinese fireworks that I keep for special occasions. Do you think Malcolm and Angus would be pleased?"

"Ben, I can't think of anything that would please them more. They might be a little embarrassed at all the attention but I think they'd both be delighted! Just tell me what I can do to help!"

"My staff will take care of everything. You just enjoy your meal tonight. Also, Jack Goodnite told me that room 5-A is vacant. If you wish, you can stay there tonight. Then Malcolm can join you there tomorrow. You will be my guests", Ben said.

Steffi gladly accepted his offer, then spent the rest of the evening chatting with the never-ending crowd that milled around their table. It was almost as though the party had already begun.

At 3:50 PM the next afternoon, old Number 88's deafening whistle signaled her approach to Alexander. Steffi and Ben, accompanied a large crowd of townsfolk and a small brass band assembled by Shorty for the occasion, were already waiting at the depot, eager for a glimpse of their heroes.

Su Chang, looking drawn and haggard from her ordeal, but jubilant to be back home, was the first to exit, swinging down into Ben's outstretched arms as the crowd cheered.

They quieted momentarily as Rolf stepped down. He was followed by Angus who exited gingerly. He was nursing two ribs that were broken when Su Chang had crashed into him.

Then Malcolm, his eye heavily bandaged, appeared before the hushed crowd. In a moment the shouting began when Shorty's band struck up "Roll Out The Barrel!"

Red faced, Malcolm waved to the crowd, then stepped down to pull Steffi's face up to his.

"Big party at the Inn! Starts at 6:00. Gonna' honor all of you!" Raymond hollered over the din, tugging on Malcolm's shirt tail to get his attention.

Up the street they all went like conquering heroes, the band switching to "Tramp! Tramp! Tramp! The Boys Are Marching!" as that was all they could play by ear.

Steffi, hanging tightly onto Malcolm's arm, shouted in his ear, "Ben's putting us up in one of the hotel rooms tonight! We've got almost two hours to clean up and get ready for the party! And I've got to tell you about the gunfight we had out at the ranch!"

Malcolm, hearing mention of that for the first time said, "A gunfight! Are you serious? You bet, I've got to hear about that. We need a little time alone--actually, maybe a lot of time!" he grinned as he squeezed her waist.

They were able to break away from the crowd at the Inn. In their room they found clean bedding and tubs filled with hot water carried up earlier by Raymond.

"I'm goin' to start soakin,'" Malcolm said, throwing his dirty clothing in the corner. "Tell me about your trouble at the ranch, then I'll tell you all about Mesa Verde."

"Honey, we've got two tubs here so I'll do a little soaking too!" Steffi exclaimed as she slid into another tub full of hot suds.

Two hours later, they entered the restaurant, once again to a standing ovation as Ben and Su Chang escorted them to the head table. They joined Angus and Rolf who were already seated.

Over the previous two hours, Ben had gotten all the information he needed from his wife to provide a detailed account of her captivity and rescue. The crowd wanted to hear everything so he related her experiences to them. It was a graphic report of the rescue efforts, enthralling his patrons from beginning to end.

When he finished, one of the cowboys shouted out to Malcolm, "Hey Malcolm! "You didn't leave that bearskin out in Colorado to rot did you?"

"That bearskin is over at the freight depot right now. It'll make a great rug for someone. Just needs to be tanned." Malcolm answered, then turned to Ben. "What do you think if we auctioned it off here tonight? We can give the proceeds to the widow's and orphan's fund over at the bank."

"Splendid, that's a splendid idea!" Ben endorsed the idea and flipped a quarter to Raymond who was cleaning tables. "Here, run over and get that bearskin, Raymond. We're going to have an auction after we eat!"

The steer, turning on the spit out back, was ready to eat. At Ben's signal, Steffi and Su Chang led the revelers onto the patio area to fill their plates. The feasting went on for almost three hours as new arrivals continued to pour in. Even Jim and Molly showed up. "When Grandma Mason heard about the party, she and Grandpa picked up the boys and took them over to their house. Told us to get ourselves over here and have a good time!" Molly reported to Steffi who always had fun when Molly was around. "So, here we are!"

"Well, hang on to your hat! Ben's got quite a party going on! He's sparing no expense!" Steffi advised.

When everyone had their fill Ben clapped his hands. The band, now playing from sheet music, opened with a rousing polka as the floor was cleared for dancing.

After two hours or so of non-stop polka-ing, it was time for a break and Ben called for the bearskin.

There was much oohing and aahing as Raymond, with help from a cowhand, stretched out the huge hide for everyone to see.

A call went out for Big Jim Kincaid to cry the auction, a task he gladly accepted.

Spirited bidding drove the price up until only two bidders were left. Chester was bidding for the bank and Jack Goodnite bid for the Inn. The bidding was hot and heavy for a while. Then, worried about spending bank funds foolishly, Chester grudgingly dropped out. Jack got himself a bearskin, and the widow's and orphan's fund was several hundred dollars richer, much to everyone's delight!

The band cranked up again as a caller stepped out and the square dancing began. Three hours later even the hardiest dancers were slowing down. Everyone headed out back and watched the fireworks display--a spectacular presentation staged by Ben. Finally, as the wee hours of dawn approached, the revelers, somewhat melancholy at seeing the festivities ending, began drifting away toward their respective homes leaving Ben's crew to do the cleaning and locking up.

The Frazier's, totally exhausted from the day's activities, went straight to bed. Just before she dozed off, Steffi remembered what Chester had asked her to do and said, "Honey, we've got something to talk about in the morning. Chester wants you to serve on the bank board." She wasn't sure Malcolm heard her. He was just beginning to snore.

Several hundred miles to the west, Peg Leg Charlie was boarding a train in Trinidad, en route to Alexander.

He would arrive there at about 4:00 PM the following day.

CHAPTER 25

THE OPPORTUNITY

J. T. Smith was stocking shelves in the back of his store when Peg Leg Charlie walked in.

"Peg Leg!" J. T. exclaimed, pumping his hand in greeting. "I got your telegram telling about Smooth Mouth and the boys. Boy, that was terrible! I really liked that old man. I never met his sons but I'll bet they were all right boys. But, what brings you back here?"

"J. T. I saw the killings take place. Not only that, I stuck around fer awhile and learned a lot about the mine. Found out things that'll interest you. I guess you own the mine now that Smooth Mouth is dead?" he asked.

"Actually, I don't," J. T. replied. "I owed the bank so much money that I gave 'em the mine shares to wipe out my debt. Chester Zimmerman and Ben Wang are the major stockholders of the bank. As such, they own the mine."

"Well, maybe I'd better high tail it over and meet the banker. I don't even know him."

"Zimmerman's the president but he's out of town for a day or two. You need to see Ben Wang. He operates the restaurant over at Goodnite's Inn. I'd take you over there and introduce you myself but I've got to get home and see my wife," he said, holding up a bottle of castor oil. "She's sicker'n a dog with the flu. If you got the time, stop back tomorrow. I really want to hear your whole story."

A few minutes later, Ben Wang looked up from his work to see a waitress escorting the old prospector to his table.

"Ben, this fellow wants to talk to you," she said as Ben rose to greet his visitor.

"They call me Peg Leg Charlie," Peg Leg said as he shook

165

Ben's hand. "I'm the one that saw the murders down at the Rose Pit mine."

"Oh yes," Ben responded enthusiastically. "I know who you are. Please have a seat."

"Well, I've got a story that'll interest you. I understand from J. T. that you're a part owner of the mine. Do you have any idea what's down there?" Peg Leg asked.

Ben, sensed that the conversation should be held private, and said, "No, I don't know much about it so I'm anxious to hear what you have to say. Why don't we go upstairs to my rooms where we can have privacy? If you haven't eaten yet, I'll have two steaks sent up for us."

"I'd be proud to eat one of them. I could smell 'em cookin' clean down to the depot. Really set my mouth to a'waterin'."

Upstairs, Peg Leg told of his experiences at the mine.

"Peg Leg," Ben said as their steaks were being served, "I've got a friend who needs to hear this story. He will find it very interesting. Would you be willing to stay in town until I can arrange a meeting? I'll pay you full wages for your time and will put you up here at the Inn. Also I'll reimburse you for your train fare out here."

"Why, shore. I ain't doin' nothin' anyhow, and you sure serve darn good vittles here. Only a dang fool would turn down a deal like that!" Peg Leg cried out, happy to be back in civilization for a few days."

That evening Ben wrote a lengthy note to Malcolm. When he was finished, he sealed it with wax and carried it to the barbershop where he found Raymond cleaning and shining boots for the hotel guests.

"Raymond, I need this note delivered to Malcolm at his ranch tonight. Could you find time to do that?" he asked, holding up a silver dollar.

"Take me five minutes to finish this last pair of boots then I'm on my way!" Raymond responded as he took the money. "Do you want me to take the gelding?"

"That will be fine. You know where I keep him."

It took less than an hour to get to the ranch. The whole family was playing on the front porch when Raymond rode up.

"What's goin' on?" Malcolm asked.

The boy handed him the note. "Ben sent this out. Wants to see you."

"Water your horse and give him some oats. Then come on inside. We're going to have supper pretty soon," Malcolm said while slitting the wax seal with his pocketknife. He was curious. *What's Ben got on his mind?*

He read: "Dear Malcolm. I am writing to you as a friend. By now you may know that the bank board is going to offer you a directorship due to the vacancy caused by J. T. Smith's resignation. You should consider that offer very carefully. Today, a man came to see me with important information that you should be aware of. He will be in town for a few days as my guest. We propose that you either come to town, or we can come out to the ranch, so you can meet him and hear his story. If agreeable, please express your wishes to Raymond regarding a time and place for a meeting. Sincerely, Ben."

Malcolm read it over again, then carefully folded it, placed it in his shirt pocket and went in to join the others for supper.

Steffi was serving ham hock and beans with cornbread. Malcolm took a seat and said, "Ben wants to have a little visit with me about some business over at the bank." Then he turned to Raymond, "Raymond, when you get back, you can tell Ben I'll come in and have breakfast with him tomorrow."

The next morning, Malcolm tied up at the hitching post and entered the busy restaurant.

"Malcolm," Ben greeted him in the foyer, "This is Peg Leg Charlie. He's the man who sent the message to J. T. about the shootings at the Rose Pit Mine. He has valuable information for us. Let us go upstairs. Our breakfast will be up shortly."

While they were waiting on their food, Ben told Malcolm that the mine stock that J. T. turned over to the bank could present some unique financial opportunities. Then he asked Peg Leg to relate his story to Malcolm.

The prospector went into great detail, leaving nothing to the imagination as he told his tale.

"So the claim jumpers think the government will buy all that copper," Malcolm said when Peg Leg finished. Then he asked. "Wonder if there's any truth to that?"

Ben answered before Peg Leg could respond, "Malcolm, I have some information regarding the government's interest that I can show you after while."

"Good, I'd like to see it," Malcolm replied. Then, turning again to Peg Leg, he asked, "You say you found a strange contract that Levi signed in Mexico. Do you have it with you?"

Peg Leg produced the document and laid it on the table.

Malcolm read it and said, "Looks like an ol' boy named Don Diego's got a whole Mexican family indebted to him and they're havin' to work off the debt. This contract says that if Levi can come up with enough to pay off the debt this year that Diego will release the family to him. Levi must've thought a lot of those people for some reason. Does look like a mighty strange agreement. Well, I guess we'll cross that bridge when we get to it."

After Peg Leg was finished with his story, Ben suggested he enjoy himself downstairs at the hotel lounge where poker and domino games were already beginning. "We might want to talk to you again soon so you might let us know if you decide to leave town for any reason," he said as he saw Peg Leg to the door.

He returned, handed Malcolm a newspaper, and said, "I've got a copy of an article here that you need to read. It verifies the fact that the government will be probably be buying millions of dollars worth of copper for a transatlantic cable."

"Boy!" Malcolm exclaimed as he read the paper. "Someone is going to get rich on this deal!"

"That's precisely why I wanted to talk with you. A strange set of circumstances have occurred that put our bank, and its' owners, in a very unique situation. It is also very timely that you are going to have an opportunity to join the board very soon. I don't know if you knew it or not but Edna Zimmerman, individually, owned 15,000 shares of bank stock. Since Edna was murdered, her stock now needs to be acquired by a new shareholder. Also, J. T. Smith owned 10,000 shares of bank stock. He couldn't pay the bank what he owed so he had to resign from the board and give up his bank stock. Of course, that stock isn't worth a whole lot. What is important is this: He had to turn over the mining stock that Smooth Mouth Sam had pledged to him. That gave the bank one hundred per cent ownership of the mine. Now the bank needs to replace Edna and J. T. on the board. Whoever owns the bank stock will automatically control the mining stock," Ben spoke slowly, watching Malcolm's eyes to see his reaction.

"Some time back when the bank needed another investor to round out the board," Ben continued, "they offered me the 30,000 shares that were available at that time. I purchased all of them. Now that Edna is gone, Chester only owns his 15,000 shares. With my 30,000 shares, I have become the major stockholder in the bank."

"This is getting interesting. Keep right on talking. I'm all ears," Malcolm said, realizing that the opportunity of a lifetime could be unfolding before him.

"The logical buyer for Edna's bank shares is Chester. But, we all know he is stretched to his limit financially because he made a lot of personal loans to ranchers who can't repay him right now. Here's where you and Steffi fit in. First of all, you risked your life to save Su Chang and there is no way I can repay that. But, I can try. Also, Steffi has become a dear friend and was there when Su Chang was captured. We owe her a lot. Her friendship with Su Chang is more important than you will ever know."

"Ben, we don't do these things expecting to get paid for them. Steffi is Su Chang's friend because she likes her. I volunteered to go to Colorado because I felt it was the thing to do. You'd have done the same for us!" Malcolm exclaimed.

"I understand," Ben continued, "and I thank you for feeling

169

that way. But let me explain my proposal to you. First of all, as an Oriental--an outsider--I am uncomfortable at having the controlling interest in the bank and would like to have someone with an equal number of shares on the board. Since two more directors are needed, why don't you fill one vacancy and Steffi fill the other? I'm sure the current board would agree to that, especially when they realize that your shares will equal mine."

"I don't quite see how we could be equal since you have 30,000 shares now and there are only 25,000 for sale; 15,000 from Edna's estate and 10,000 from J. T.'s interest," Malcolm inquired.

Ben replied, "That is a problem I've considered. It can be solved very easily. I will sell you enough of my shares so we will be equal. You and Steffi will have a vote equal to mine."

"What's Chester goin' to think about all of this?" Malcolm asked. "I realize he doesn't control the board, but after all, he's the founder and president of the bank."

"Well, that brings up a very confidential issue, Malcolm," Ben's voice dropped to a conspiratorial tone. "You've probably heard that Chester is out of town on business. Only the board members know that he has gone to Kansas City for a check up. Since Edna died, he has not felt well. Last week, he had such stomach pains that he missed two days work. The board of directors practically ordered him to go see a doctor."

"Gosh, is he really that bad?" Malcolm asked.

"We think so. But to answer your question about his concern for the bank, his interest in the business certainly isn't what it used to be. I seriously doubt if he would have any objection whatsoever to you and I sharing control of the bank. I think all he wants to do is hang on to his job, if, in fact his health will even allow for that," Ben answered.

Malcolm responded, "Ben, you certainly know how to get a man to think! Let's assume that Steffi and I agree and are put on the board. Looks to me like about the first order of business will be to figure out how to get control of the mine and start operating it. I don't know how we could do that from here."

"The situation presents a variety of problems," Ben replied. "First of all, the mine practically straddles the Mexico-U.S. border. It's sort of in no-man's land. We've wired various law offices in the region about the possibility of getting help to arrest the claim jumpers. After all, they did kill three men. But, nobody seems to have, or wants to have, jurisdiction down there. Southeastern Arizona is a long way from anywhere. Also, with the large number of border skirmishes going on with Mexico, the army is occupied. They would help if they had the manpower and time. Right now, they don't. I think our little bank is going to have to figure out a solution on it's own. That's another reason why I want you on the board. We need all the good minds that we can find."

"You know, Ben, I've been listenin' pretty good. Seems to me like it'll take quite a bit of time for us to get organized and we'll need a lot of information that could be tough to come by. Maybe old Peg Leg can help out."

"Maybe so. What do you propose?" Ben asked.

"Peg Leg mentioned that the claim jumpers need a lot more help. They're already tired of diggin' ore. Of course they don't trust anyone. Now, even though Peg Leg was down there, they never met him. He's an old prospector that looks like the kind of fellow to help 'em out. He could play the part perfectly. It he's agreeable, I think the bank ought to pay him to go down and infiltrate that operation for awhile. We need to know if the mine is actually worth workin'. We don't know for sure if we can get a government contract to buy the copper. And, we don't know if we could operate it at a profit if we took it over. It might cost more to get it out than it's worth. I always thought copper was strip mined. Peg Leg says the Rose Pit is a shaft operation and they're tunneling into the mountain. There's lots of questions to be answered before the bank gets involved. If Peg Leg was in there feeding us information, then we'd understand a lot better what our options are. What do you think?" Malcolm asked.

Ben, delighted with Malcolm's analysis, replied, "That might just work. I'll talk to Peg Leg about staying around for a

171

few days. That will give Chester time to get back. If Chester is up to it, we can call for a special meeting to get you and Steffi voted in by the board. Then we can discuss the mining situation and see if the board agrees with our ideas. Personally, I think sending Peg Leg down there is the only thing to do! It'll buy us a lot of valuable time!"

"There's just one more big stumbling block I can see," Malcolm said. "Suppose Peg Leg takes us up on our proposition and goes to work at the mine. We've got to figure a way for him to get messages back to us. He won't have access to a telegraph and they aren't goin' to let him out of sight. If he can't keep us informed, there is no use in sending him down there."

Ben nodded, "You've got a point. We'll have to come up with a solution."

"I've got a couple of ideas," Malcolm said. "If I decide they're worth considering, I'll bring 'em up at the board meeting. I need to think about it. They might not work."

Malcolm started back to the Wandering S. Five miles from home, his mind was made up. He detoured off the main trail, disappeared into a deep ravine and followed it for two miles. He came to ramshackle hut barely visible in the brush. Out back, dozens of wire cages cluttered the yard. An old man dressed in rags was standing in the doorway. His rifle was leveled at Malcolm's head.

"Don't get your bowels in an uproar, Silas!" Malcolm hollered, hold out his hands to show he wasn't armed. "I'm down here to talk business."

Two hours later, he was home. He rode to the barn and started grooming his mare with a currycomb.

Steffi walked out. She noticed he had brought two pigeons home and confined them in a coop. "What'd you do? Bring the boys home some birds to play with?"

"No, they're part of my master plan. They're not to even know they're here. But, right now, I've got an important question for you. How'd you like to be married to a millionaire? Think you could handle that?"

"Sounds good!" Steffi replied, going along with the little joke. "Who is my new husband going to be?"

"Nobody. You're stuck with me. But, first," he said as Steffi, her mouth gaping, began to listen with interest, "we've got to make you a director and partner in the First State Bank of Alexander. That's what we've got to do!"

CHAPTER 26

IN THE CAMP OF THE ENEMY

Bob and Sy were worn out. For weeks they'd wielded their heavy picks twelve hours a day piling up tons of ore as they clawed away at the rich vein. The problem was, they had no buyers. If the government was in the market it hadn't put out the word yet. The exhausted men began to doubt their own judgment as the back-breaking labor took its toll. They drank heavily and their tempers exploded over minor disagreements. And there were three graves to haunt them, grim reminders of their crimes. Lack of water created another problem. It had to be hauled over several rugged miles so they rationed it and only bathed once a week. The nighttime was agonizing. They slept fitfully, their tortured minds flooded with memories of men rolling in the dirt, unable to escape the lead slugs ripping their bodies. Sweating and stinking in their filthy bunks, they counted the hours until the cool night air would replace the blazing desert heat. The desert was slow to yield its stifling embrace and the hot nights drug on. They tried late night poker games and sips from their jug of white lightnin', but nothing relieved their misery.

It was into this environment of high tension and despair that Peg Leg Charlie appeared, meandering along, leading two donkeys loaded with prospecting tools and grub. He said he was just looking for a few days work with enough pay to get himself on down the trail.

It wasn't yet noon, but as the outlaws questioned him, Peg Leg could see that Sy had been drinking heavily from the bottle lying nearby.

When he looked into their eyes, he chilled as he met their empty stare. Years earlier, he'd seen the same, vacant look in the eyes of a prisoner on death row. He shuddered now as he'd shuddered then, knowing his life wasn't worth ten cents if they discovered his motive.

Bob asked, "Do you know how to shoot dynamite? We need a dynamite man."

"Made a livin' at it for quite a few years. It don't scare me none."

"OK, we'll hire you at two dollars a day. We'll double that on the days you shoot dynamite. Ain't neither one of us goin' to touch the stuff, so you'll make some money."

They walked into the tiny mine shack.

"Where do I bunk?" Peg Leg asked. "I've got a tent."

"You can sleep outside if you want to. Just pitch it next to us. We like to keep track of anybody workin' for us."

"How come you haul those pigeons around with you?" Bob had asked, seeing a coop holding two birds tied on the back of a donkey.

"I always carry a mascot with me. Used to have a falcon named King but he died so I picked up these pigeons," Peg Leg answered. "I call 'em Pancho and Rosa 'cause I got 'em down in Mexico."

"Keep 'em cooped up," Sy ordered. "I hate the filthy things. To me, they're just good fer target practice. I can knock one out of the air with my .44. I've done it many a time."

"These birds don't hurt nobody. They just fly at night and always come back," Peg Leg was alarmed, knowing that their death would doom his mission.

Two weeks later, Malcolm was in the corral when he heard Steffi calling from the barn, "Hey, Pancho's back! He's got a message on his leg band!"

Sure enough, there was Pancho sitting on a perch with a message from Peg Leg.

Using dynamite. Tremendous vein of copper. Rumor that government will pay top dollar. Tempers hot here. They may hire more workers and gunmen to defend the mine. Come soon, ready to fight!

176

"Honey, if we're goin' to get rich, it looks like we'll have to work for it. Maybe fight for it," Malcolm was sobered by the note. "I'd better get into town and talk with the others. May need a special board meeting just to see how deep the bank wants to get into this thing. I'll send back a note to Peg Leg with an A written on it. That means acknowledged and he'll know we got the message."

Malcolm picked up Ben in the morning and they headed straight to the bank.

Chester was alone in his office. He read the note, handed it back to Malcolm and said, "Boys it looks like you're going to have a fight on your hands if you're going to take over that mine. And it's going to be your fight, not mine. I just got a wire from the clinic in Kansas City this morning."

He handed them the wire from his doctor. They read it. Their jaws tensed and they handed it back.

"Chester, this doesn't sound too good. What do you plan to do?" Malcolm asked in a hushed voice.

"Well, if the malignancy hasn't spread too far, they'll probably operate. It's in my abdominal area, they can't tell just where. In any event, I want to go back east for the operation. If I survive, Dad will have a place for me in his bank. I think the fair thing to do is to resign my position here and let you fellows get on with bringing on a new president. You've got a lot of problems to face and I won't be of any help. A lot of starch went out of me when Edna died. Now I've got to fight this through. It just seems like it's high time for me to move on." Chester's voice cracked, evidence of his weakened physical and emotional condition.

"Chester, I think I can speak for the board when I say we do not want to see you go. Is their no alternative, or is your mind made up?" Ben asked, his eyes searching for an answer.

"Ben, I appreciate that. I really do, but, yes, my mind is made up. Actually, I don't have much choice when you examine the whole issue."

He nodded at Malcolm and continued, "I'll be leaving the

bank in good shape now that you and Steffi are on the board. You fellows can buy my bank stock. I doubt if the other directors care since they're in minority positions with or without it. The new president you hire can take my place on the board. He may want some stock and you'll have it available."

Malcolm and Ben glanced at each other. It was obvious that Chester was resigned to his fate.

"Are you up to convening a special meeting of the board in the next few days?" Malcolm asked. "Looks like we've got some serious business to discuss."

"Sure. I'll set it up as quick as I can."

Chester chaired his final meeting at 4PM the following day. Jack Goodnite, Jess Monts and George Norton were in attendance along with Malcolm, Steffi, and Ben.

Chester explained his illness and tendered his resignation, stating that he would be leaving town within a week. Goodnite, Monts, and Norton were visibly disturbed. They had no idea that he was so sick. Chester suggested they name their loan officer, Bill Peaseman, to the position of acting president until the job was filled. He then turned the meeting over to his Vice Chairman, George Norton, and excused himself saying it would serve no purpose for him to set through their discussions.

After he left, they talked about his situation for several minutes, regretting the fact that his health and dreams were unraveling just when things were looking up. They took his advice and agreed to offer the acting president's job to Bill Peaseman.

A lively discussion about the bank's interest in the Rose Pit Mine followed.

The others were content to let Ben and Malcolm do most of the talking since they had the most to gain, and, the most to lose.

"Peg Leg sent this message to us a couple of days ago by carrier pigeon. That's the only way we can communicate," Malcolm said, holding up the note. "I don't know exactly what we should do. If we knew for sure that the government was goin' to start buying great quantities of copper, we'd have something to go on. Ben got an article out of the paper that indicates they might just do that, but things are still a little uncertain. Why don't you pass that article around, Ben, so everyone can read it? "

George Norton read the items. "You're right," he said. "We could go running down to Arizona and get ourselves killed over some ore and not have a buyer for it. I'm dead set against doing anything until we actually know what the market is for the copper! What do the rest of you think?"

Jess Monts, usually the quiet director, spoke up. "Well, that only makes good sense. We can't be running around like a bunch of dang chickens with our heads cut off. Maybe I can help solve our problem. My wife has a cousin in Virginia that's married to a congressman. Name's Frank Peck. If I get a hold of him, I'll bet he can tell us all about the government's interest in copper. In fact, if we wait two weeks, we can talk to him in person. Him and Penelope, that's my wife's cousin, are goin' to California for a month and are goin' to stop here and see us for a couple of days. That-a-way we can get it straight from the horses mouth."

Mont's idea was well received.

"Might be wise to send a wire and let him know of our interest. That way he can come prepared," Norton advised.

Mont agreed and the meeting adjourned.

Down at the Rose Pit Mine, Peg Leg was feeling the pressure. The message from Malcolm acknowledged receipt but offered no plan of action and the situation was rapidly deteriorating. Sy and Bob, burned out as miners and totally disgusted with the whole miserable situation, piled on more and more hard work. They spent their time nursing whiskey bottles and target shooting at anything that moved. To top it off, Peg Leg hadn't been paid and was being treated like a slave. Sy told him that he'd get paid when they did. The one time he'd inquired about the three graves out front, interested in hearing how they would explain their presence, he'd received a chilling response from Bob. "Ain't nothin' buried there but three old donkeys. We shot 'em when we took over the mine. Had to bury 'em deep to keep the coyotes away. Fact is, Sy says if he hears much more braying out of yours while he's trying to sleep, there'll soon be two more graves. Three more if you don't like it."

Bob had grinned as he jacked a live round into his Winchester, and then fixed his sights on Peg Leg's head.

"Never did care much for you, old man," he'd laughed, taunting Peg Leg. "Why don't you just give me an excuse and we'll see how much hot lead your head can absorb. I'll bet it's a bunch!"

"Hey! Don't kill him yet. We got tons of ore to dig! I ain't about to do it myself and you're too drunk to work. Let him live 'till we're done!" Sy hollered. "Here, have a drink. Leave the old man alone, for now! Hee Ha! Let him work! He'll be our ticket out of here yet!"

Peg Leg was in a tough spot and he didn't like it. All he could do was hope and pray that Malcolm would round up a posse and get him out fast. He figured he probably didn't have two weeks to live the way things were going.

CHAPTER 27

THE WAITING GAME

"Honey! Pancho showed up again this morning with another message! This time, it looks like Peg Leg is in serious trouble!" Steffi ran out and handed the note to Malcolm as he rode in for his noon meal.

He took the note and saw the cause of her alarm: Dangerous here. Lots of whiskey and gunplay. Threatening me and my animals. I am a slave. They're going crazy. Doubt if I can hold on for two weeks.

"Boy, he's in deep trouble," Malcolm said. "We need to get 'im out of there, but now isn't the time. It'll be more than a week before the congressman gets here. Tell you what. I'll send a message back and let him know we're working on the situation. Just hope it doesn't get intercepted. If it does, he's dead."

"Wait a minute! I don't like that idea," Steffi exclaimed. "It's too dangerous. I think we're taking undue risk with his life. It's one thing for him to send us messages. It's something else when we start writing back. What if they intercept our pigeon?"

"Well, what can we do? We've got to reassure him somehow or he's goin' to come apart on us."

Steffi answered, "It sounds like the claim jumpers are tired of hard work. That's why they hired him. Maybe they need another hired hand. Why don't we send someone else down there? I'll bet they'd hire just about anyone. That's the best way to help Peg Leg."

"Well, that's a great idea but I only know of one man in town who'd take on that assignment. And I'd hate to ask him to do it."

"You're talking about Angus."

"Right. But how could I ask him to do this? He's still got bandaged ribs from our escapade in Mesa Verde."

181

"Angus can shovel more rock with one hand than any three other men put together! Besides, he's a good friend of Peg Leg and would be insulted if you didn't ask him to go. We could put him on the bank's payroll and he can probably use the money. Most important, he's the only man in town with enough guts to walk into a situation as dangerous as that."

"Everything you say is right. I just hate to ask him. But, we don't have too many choices. I'll ride in this afternoon and talk to Ben and the others. It they agree, then I'll talk to Angus. In the meantime, we've got to send a message back with Pancho, something that won't get Peg Leg in trouble if it's intercepted," Malcolm said.

They went inside and he wrote one line: <u>You are a good man, Mr. Fortnight</u>.

"What does that mean?" Steffi asked. "How can he get anything out of that?"

"As you well know, Peg Leg has quite a British accent," Malcolm explained. "He was in his teens before his parents moved over here. In England, they say fortnight when they mean two weeks. He'll know that we plan action within that time period. If the claim jumpers intercept it they won't know what it's all about and Peg Leg can slough it off as though some prankster caught the pigeon and attached the note. He can plead ignorance and they'll never be the wiser."

Pancho flew away, the message rolled and tied around his leg, and Malcolm left for town.

Throughout the day he talked to each board member and encountered no objection in asking for Angus' help.

When Malcolm presented the proposition, Angus asked, "Why not? Sounds like a lot more fun than blacksmithing and the pay is certainly a lot better!"

That evening, he left on the train to Trinidad. From there, he'd take the stagecoach to Tombstone, outfit himself with used prospecting tools, buy a couple of mules or donkeys, and head on down to the mine.

When Pancho flew into Peg Leg's tent, the message he

carried brought a smile to Peg Leg's face. 'Fortnight' stuck out like a sore thumb. Help would be coming soon.

A few days later, he was coming out of the mine and heard Sy yell, "Hey! Bob! Take a look! What have we got here?"

Peg Leg looked out and saw a bear of a man leading two scraggly pack mules wandering toward camp.

Bob, ever vigilante, levered a steel jacketed round into his Winchester and said, "I don't know, but if he wants a job, hire 'im! He looks like he could move a mountain by hisself!"

Peg Leg walked out into the sunshine. He felt like jumping sky high when he recognized Angus.

He kept his calm but his mind raced. *It's the blacksmith from Alexander! Malcolm sent him!*

Angus showed no sign of recognition as he ambled over to talk with Sy and Bob. They hired him on the spot, marveling at his size and obvious strength, believing he could triple the output from the mine.

That night, Angus pitched his tent nearby. When Sy and Bob collapsed after finishing their last bottle of the day, he crept into Peg Leg's tent.

"Boy, you're a sight for sore eyes!" Peg Leg greeted him. "I don't figger I could last another week with these yahoos. They're gunhappy and me'n my animals is all they got to shoot at."

"Malcolm got your messages and we knew you were in trouble," Angus said, then told him about the meeting coming up with the congressman. He continued, "If the government guarantees a high enough price, Malcolm'll bring enough men down here to take over the mine. If the government story is all hog-wash and there ain't no market for the copper, well, in that case, we'll just shoot our way out of here if we have to and head on home. We should know somethin' in about two weeks, so we've got to hang on for awhile."

On Saturday night, Congressman Frank Peck and his wife Penelope stepped off the train at Alexander.

A luncheon at Ben's restaurant, a reception of sorts for the visiting dignitaries, was hosted by the bank board at noon on Sunday--an event attended by all board members.

The word spread fast causing the majority of the townspeople to decide that they too needed to have Sunday dinner at Ben's place.

By three that afternoon, everybody who was anybody and a lot of people who weren't, had greeted the new arrivals, enthusiastically expressed their political opinions, and had gone away, boasting the fact that they'd shaken hands with a congressman.

Only then were the guests and their hosts allowed to adjourn in peace to the only drawing room in rural Kansas. The women enjoyed tea and desert while the men lit cigars and drank the rich, black coffee brewed by Ben for special occasions.

For about three hours, Frank and Penelope had been under close scrutiny. They had created a wonderful impression, gaining the approval of the townsfolk as they basked in the warm hospitality.

Frank exuded a genuine confidence that put everyone at ease. He was tall and slender with a mane of silver hair. His suite was a three-piece navy blue pin stripe, tailored to compliment his physique. Gray spats, the mark of an eastern gentleman, adorned his patent leather shoes. He cut an impressive figure but wasn't pompous and didn't intimidate his hosts. He was obviously a man of integrity, able to deal with a wide range of issues important to the growing nation.

Everyone's ears perked up when he mentioned that he was educated as a lawyer and handled legal matters for the Western States Banking Association prior to entering politics.

He had another great asset; Penelope. She was a Georgia Peach if there ever was one. Her very presence displayed the charm of her blue blood heritage. Her blond hair cascaded over her yellow chiffon party dress. Her clothing was of high fashion, worthy of a Washington ballroom, yet, worn in good taste in little Alexander. She revealed that she'd attended finishing school in Charleston even though her family lost their plantation during the war.

They had two daughters; twins age two, who were staying at home with their grandparents.

Frank had first worked in Washington as a lawyer on a variety of complicated legal matters for the government as it began the reconstruction of the South.

As the afternoon wore on, the subject all of them were most interested in came up.

"The rumors and articles are real," Frank responded in answer to Malcolm's question about the planned transatlantic cable. "It'll stretch from the east coast to London and will use all the copper that can be found. Right now, not a lot is available so no contracts have been let. Congress wants to find a prime source of supply before they get the country all worked up. Jess tells me you may have a line on a producing mine. I can assure you, Washington will be interested, especially if the mine can become a major producer."

"You know, perhaps this discussion should be held over at our bank," Ben said, always alert to the need for privacy.

"Good idea," George Norton agreed, then turned to Frank and Penelope. "Maybe we ought to let these good folks get some rest tonight. Then we'd be glad to have you over for a meeting at the bank tomorrow morning."

A meeting was set for 10 AM. Everyone drifted away except for Malcolm and Steffi who lingered over their drinks with Ben.

"You know," Malcolm opened up, "I really like Frank and his wife. A man like him could be of invaluable help with his knowledge of government contracts and banking procedures. What do you think about him?"

"Malcolm," Ben's enthusiasm bubbled to the surface, "I've never seen anyone so qualified to help us! I don't know what his political future is, but, if the opportunity presents itself, we should make a strong effort to get him to head up the bank since Chester's leaving. Probably the salary we can offer won't sway him, but we can see to it that he gets Chester's stock. If the mine comes along like it should, the stock can make him, as well as us, independently wealthy. The question, as I see it, will be: 'What is his long term goal in the political arena'?"

"That's probably the key factor. At our meeting tomorrow, we've got to really open up with this man. If we get lucky, and I mean really lucky, we might just get his attention!" Malcolm replied.

In the meantime, the mood was changing at the Rose Pit Mine.

Sy had just ridden in from Tombstone with a supply of fresh grub and a dozen jars of home brew.

"Lookee here!" he called to Bob as he dismounted, holding aloft a copy of a Phoenix newspaper. "We may not be so dumb after all!"

Bob wasn't very smart but he could read. The article, written by an Arizona reporter, was less than a week old. It reported that the Arizona Territory was loaded with copper and the government was soon going to be buying a lot of it, assumedly for the construction of a transatlantic cable.

"What do we do now?" Bob asked, always seeking direction.

"Well, first of all, let's don't get stupid!" Sy, his head pounding from his daily hangover, replied. "We're goin' to make our men dig like their pants are on fire! And, if any more show up lookin' fer a job, we'll put them to work! Now's the time to hit it hard! I'll guarantee you; we're going to get rich! It's just going to take a little more time."

Peg Leg and Angus could overhear bits and pieces of the conversation.

Angus whispered, "Maybe now these gun crazy drunks'll leave us alone. Killing or wounding us now would be the height of stupidity."

They would not have slept so well that night if they'd heard the conversation between Sy and Bob in the mine shack.

"I don't trust our diggers. Don't know why, but it just looks to me like they're a lot smarter than most prospectors I ever ran into. If we get a chance to hire some replacements, I think old Peg Leg and Angus'll probably just disappear in a mine explosion."

That'll solve our problem," Bob grinned at the idea. "It looks like the only thing to do."

Ernest C. Frazier

CHAPTER 28

THE ALEXANDER/WASHINGTON CONNECTION

Malcolm and Steffi could hardly sleep as they considered the opportunities created if Congressman Peck came in as president of the bank.

"We are absolutely looking at a gold mine--whoops!--in this case, a copper mine," Malcolm corrected his statement but Steffi caught the drift. "The problem is, without Frank or somebody else with his knowledge and connections, our chances of taking over the mine and working out a deal with the government are about zero. We could take some men down there, capture or shoot down the claim jumpers--whichever we have to do--and take over. I don't have any doubt about that. But then, we'd have to raise a lot of capital to get into big time production. We couldn't raise the money to do that unless we had the ore contracted to the government and were guaranteed a profit on delivery. Frank's the only one who can arrange those contracts. None of the rest of us has the political connections to pull it off. At least, nowhere in the near future. I guess what I'm saying is this. Without Frank, this deal isn't going anywhere, at least not in our lifetimes."

Steffi was sitting upright in the bed. She slumped a bit with Malcolm's last statement. "You mean we stand to lose the whole opportunity if Frank doesn't get involved? All of this effort, plus risking Peg Leg and Angus, wouldn't amount to anything in that case. Well, I think we'd just better figure out a way to make certain that Frank comes on board, even if he has to sacrifice his political career! Any ideas?"

"I'm thinking that the base pay for a congressman is pretty meager compared to owning fifteen percent of a bank--Ben and I would sell him that much--that controls one hundred percent of a

189

mine that should soon be worth millions. If power and prestige are what he wants out of life and money is a secondary issue, then he would probably choose to stay in political life. Especially if he thinks he might make it all the way to the top. And, we have to agree; he looks like a man that could govern the whole nation if he had the chance. On the other hand, he may be sick of politics and wants out. Who knows, money may be more important to him than power. I guess we'll find out tomorrow. But, you hit the nail on the head. We just can't afford to let him get away! I think we'd consider anything within reason to get him to stay here. Huh! Let's face it. We might even go beyond reason!"

Downtown at the Goodnite Inn, Ben and Su Chang were having a similar discussion. Neither couple slept well that night.

Shortly after 10 AM the group assembled at the bank. Coffee and cinnamon rolls were sent over from the restaurant, setting the stage for an informal discussion, hopefully leading to a formal meeting in the near future.

George Norton, whose knowledge of the situation at the mine was limited, suggested that Ben and Malcolm brief Frank on the situation.

The discussion went on for about an hour, no thought being left unspoken as all the board members wanted Frank and Penelope to be able to envision the opportunity as they saw it.

As the meeting wound down, Frank took a deep breath and said, "It would be hard for me to leave Alexander without giving serious thought to your offer. You're talking about the possibility of a huge fortune for anyone owning stock in this bank. I realize the board hasn't formally offered me the bank presidency, but as I understand it, that's what you have in mind if I'm interested. Do I understand you correctly?"

"That is correct," Ben responded. "If you want the position, and the board concurs by majority vote, which should be no problem, it will be yours."

All present, including Penelope, held their breaths as Frank continued, "I must say, from what you've stated here, I have more than casual interest. But, let me ask you this; From what I hear, none of you have actually seen the Rose Pit Mine in person. Is that a fact?"

"That's right," Malcolm answered. "We are going on what's been reported to us. None of us have been there."

"Well, before I make any decisions, I want to see the mine for myself. I want to get an idea of our being able to develop it into a major producer, probably by converting it to a strip mining operation, and see if there's any potential problems because of the location. It appears that the mine is right on the Mexican border. I know that if we got in a dispute and the property was deemed to be in Mexico, or even straddled the border, Mexico could wind up owning the mine. A surveyor could answer that question. In addition, the stock assignments look valid and it's assumed that Smooth Mouth Sam properly recorded his ownership. That needs to be verified by examining the courthouse records. That will help determine if we'll get a clear title. Those are major issues that need to be resolved whether you hire me or not."

"Frank, you have an excellent legal mind," Ben said. "It is apparent that we need a person of your background and ability to assist us with any problems that come up. Are we to understand that if you visit the area personally and determine that none the issues presents an insurmountable obstacle, that you surely would consider taking the bank presidency here?"

"You understand correctly, Ben," Frank answered, then continued with other considerations. "Politics is a rough and tumble game. There's no guarantee that I'll be re-elected in the fall even if I choose to run. My opponent has unlimited resources and comes from a family with a rich political heritage. So, by necessity I've been giving some thought to returning to the private sector. Actually, I've been considering joining one of the law firms that has boosted my career. But, the bank presidency, the bank stock, and the mining interests would take care of my financial needs for life. Just as important, it would expose my family to a much more interesting way of life here on the frontier. Here's what I propose. It's almost noon. Why don't I take Penelope back to the hotel for something to eat and you folks can talk this whole thing over in private? If the board agrees to offer me the position, then I think it's important that one of you accompany me to Arizona so we can get a close look at the mine. Our train leaves for California tomorrow. You send whoever you want to ride out with us. The train stops in Tucson. Penelope can spend some time there while we go on to the mine."

The board agreed to the proposition. The next problem was to decide who would go. That became a thorny issue. The expectation of great wealth was clouding everyone's judgment. As a result, everybody wanted to go, envisioning the trip as a great adventure.

"Drawing straws is what we'll have to do," George said. "Actually, we should exclude Malcolm 'cause he just got back from about getting himself killed out in Colorado!"

"No sir!" Malcolm objected strenuously. "That battle had nothing to do with the bank's business. I've got a lot at stake here and I'm entitled to be in on the drawing! You're not keepin' me out of this one!"

"Let's get on with it, George," Jess was resigned to the situation. "You can't tell a hardheaded Scotsman anything!"

They each took a straw. George, half kidding and half mad, yelled out, "Rigged! The drawing is rigged!" when Malcolm drew the short one. "I just knew you were goin' to win! How comes you're always so lucky? Scotsmen ain't supposed to be so lucky!"

"Luck of the Irish," Malcolm replied. "My mother was born in Belfast."

Three days later they pulled into Tucson. Penelope took rooms in the Harvey House and Frank changed into western garb. They were on a stagecoach to Tombstone before noon. It was a bone-jarring, two-day ride. As soon as they got there, Malcolm started shopping for supplies and horses. Frank went to the courthouse and found the documentation he was seeking, a paper trail proving that Smooth Mouth had an attorney record the mining claim, set up the corporation, and issue stock.

Malcolm bought two saddle horses, bedrolls, canteens, and a couple of haversacks stuffed with food. They inquired around and were directed to a real estate sales office where they found the only surveyor in the area, a bespectacled, stoop shouldered little man, probably not five feet two, who, while thin through the shoulders and hips, nevertheless had a round little paunch that protruded out over his belt line. His name was Lazlo Millershaski, an immigrant from Poland who had learned his craft working for the territorial government. He told them he charged four dollars a day plus expenses. When they told him the survey was to be conducted on the Mexican border and outside the view of those working the mine, he balked and said he wasn't interested in the job. His negativism evaporated when Malcolm held up a fifty dollar gold piece and said it would be his if he could complete the secret survey in two days.

Within an hour, they were on their way to the mine. The next morning found them a bluff overlooking the mine's entrance, scanning the area with their binoculars.

They tensed, seeing not only Angus and Peg Leg preparing to head into the shaft, but six Mexican workers, their chests crossed by bandoliers of ammunition and six guns swinging from their hips. It was obvious that, while they were recruited to work in the mine, their main function would be to defend it as they lined up, military style, to receive instructions from Sy and Bob.

"For some reason, they're puttin' on more people to increase production," Malcolm said. "Maybe they heard that the government is going to start buying soon. I don't like the looks of those hired guns. Probably deserters from Villa's army. They look like they'd kill anyone for a pot of beans and a bottle of beer. Maybe just for the beer. They carry enough firepower to hold off a small army."

"Lazlo, the minute they all get in the mine, you'd better start the survey. We need to know pronto if that mine is really in the U. S."

"I can do the survey in two days without any help. But, if one of you will help me by placing my stakes, we can do it in one day. Otherwise, it'll take two full days even if we don't get any interruptions," Lazlo responded, obviously hoping for some help with his very dangerous assignment.

"He's right. I'll help him with the survey, Frank. Why don't you keep the rifles and cover us from here? We'll have our pistols. If we're discovered, we'll try to make it to that arroyo. It's full of brush. Oh, I forgot to ask," Malcolm smiled nervously as he checked his pistol, "you are handy with a rifle, aren't you?"

"I was raised in the woods so I've shot enough squirrels and wild turkey to fill a box car. I can handle these without too much trouble," Frank answered, much to Malcolm's relief.

Malcolm peered through his glass and saw Angus and Peg Leg lighting their torches. They disappeared from view when they entered the mine with the pistoleros.

"Malcolm should've got my last message by now. Told him we ain't goin' to last too much longer," Peg Leg whispered when they were alone for a moment.

Angus trimmed a fuse and said, "If they don't show up pretty quick, I think we'd better make a run for it. Our lives aren't worth a confederate greenback now that they've got somebody else to do the diggin'. I found boot tracks around my tent so I know they are slippin' around here at night, spyin' on us to see if we're getting' together. I figure they're plannin' to do us in!"

"Doesn't sound too healthy for us, does it? Right now we're gettin' into a dangerous part of the mine. They want me to plan a series of charges along this fault," Peg Leg explained. "There ain't no problem with that as long as everybody is outside when they go off. But, I'll guarantee you one thing, if I do it right, this'll be a doozy. One blast should do it. It'll tell us whether this is a truly gigantic mine or jist another good producer. It's goin' to take me half a day jist to figure out where to place these charges to do the most good. If I'm wrong, the whole shaft caves in. It ain't no easy task."

"Well, I got to catch up with the others. I'll keep an eye on all of 'em. They may have already got the word to finish us off. I'll stay awake, you can bet on that!" Angus left and followed the bobbing lights into the darkness.

Having others to do the work, Sy and Bob returned to the shack.

Frank trained his binoculars on the window. "They're starting to drink out of a jar," he announced. "Peg Leg said they drank a lot. He wasn't kidding."

"OK," Malcolm touched Lazlo's shoulder, "we might as well head on down. I doubt if they'll come outside in this heat, not with a snoot full of hard liquor."

They slipped down the hill with their equipment, positioned themselves on the windowless side of the shack, and begin the survey.

Frank trained his rifle on the front door. Lazlo scurried around the area, directing Malcolm to position his markers.

By noon, the sun had climbed high in the cloudless sky. Fatigue set in as the heat sucked precious energy from the surveyors. When their task was about two thirds complete, they re-joined Frank for a well-deserved rest in the shade of some pinion trees. There was plenty of drinking water along with beef jerky and hard tack awaiting them.

"The problem we've got now, besides the heat which we can live with if we carry plenty of water, is going to be exposure to that window," Malcolm said between gulps. "We'll be right in their view if they look out for any reason. And we've got to go into that area to finish the survey."

A movement at the shack's front door caught their attention. "Look!" Frank exclaimed, "They're taking some grub down for the men. I saw smoke coming out of the chimney so I knew they'd been cooking. If they pick up some tools, that'll probably mean they are going to stay and work with the crew. That'll give you the time you need to finish your job."

Sy walked into the mine carrying two huge pots of stew. Bob picked up a couple of picks and shovels and followed him in.

"What do you think, Lazlo? You ready to finish up?" Malcolm asked as he refilled their canteens.

"I'm ready and we'd better move fast. I don't want to get caught out in their front yard with these tools. I'm ready if you are!"

Working without rest under the blazing sun, they were able to finish in just over two hours.

"Done," Lazlo gasped. His body was soaked with sweat. "Let's grab our stuff and get up the hill. I'll do my calculations up there. I've got all the information we need to figure out which country this mine is in."

Deep in the mine, Sy was whispering instructions. Angus and Peg Leg were not to leave alive!

Angus, as usual, labored alone, splitting out granite-like chunks of ore with his pick. Ten yards away, Sy nodded to two of the pistoleros. They took off their boots and crept in without a sound. Angus never heard them. The attack was swift and brutal. A gun butt bounced from the impact as it smashed against his skull.

They caught him before he hit the ground. It took a mighty effort, but with Bob's help, they hoisted the giant body into an ore cart. It already contained one body, as Peg Leg, who'd been felled moments earlier by an axe handle, lay unconscious, bleeding from a deep gash in his temple.

"Just dump him on top of the other one," Bob instructed. "Shove that cart as far back in the shaft as you can. Then get back here! We've got some dynamite to play with!"

On the bluff, Malcolm and Frank were trying to relax while the meticulous Lazlo checked and double checked his calculations.

Finally, the answer came.

"That mine is a good nine hundred yards on the U.S. side of the border. No doubt about it. Congratulations! You own yourselves a copper mine!"

"Boy, that's a relief!" Malcolm slapped Lazlo on the shoulder.

"Good job! Mighty good job!" Frank gripped the little surveyor's hand. "And you didn't even have to dodge any bullets!"

"We were lucky," Malcolm said. "Now I've got to figure out how to get our men out. I've got a hunch they're bein' watched pretty close at night. If we move on the mine we'll wind up in a gun battle. We're outgunned. It's not your fight and there's no reason for the two of you to get involved in that. Here's what I propose. You fellows high tail it out right now. Lazlo, you're job is done, and, it was a great job. Frank, before you head on to California, I would only ask that you send a wire back to Ben and tell him to send me at least a half dozen more men. I think that's about what we'll need to break Peg Leg and Angus out of there. I'll stick around and keep an eye on things until they get here. What do you think?"

Lazlo nodded in affirmation as Frank answered, "Well, we hate to leave you but you're probably right. There's one thing I'm convinced of. Now that we know the bank owns the mine, my mind is made up. If the board gives final approval, I'm ready to be a banker and sink my roots in Alexander!"

"There won't be any problem with the board," Malcolm replied. "You'll be voted in unanimously."

They shook hands and prepared to part company.

"Wait a minute! Look!" Lazlo cried as he swung up on his mare and got a full view of the mine entrance. "They're gettin' ready to dynamite!"

Malcolm and Frank grabbed their binoculars. Sy, Bob, and the six pistoleros were running out of the mine toward a ravine about a hundred yards away.

A moment passed. No one else came out of the mine.

197

"Oh, no!" Malcolm exclaimed and grabbed his rifle. "Peg Leg and Angus are still in there!"

Before they could react a thunderous explosion split the air. The earth heaved beneath their feet causing them to reel like drunken sailors. Lazlo's mount panicked. She bucked and pitched in a wild frenzy, sending her hapless rider face down in the dirt, leaving him to curse helplessly while she bolted from camp.

"Are you all right?" Frank helped Lazlo to his feet. "That was a nasty fall!"

"I've taken worse," Lazlo said, brushing off his clothes. "Good thing that horse headed north. She'd have given us away for sure if she ran to the mine."

Malcolm started say something but was interrupted by Frank who declared, "We can't leave now. They left our men trapped inside. If the blast didn't kill 'em, they're sealed inside and may still have a chance. We've got to stick around and try to get 'em out!"

Lazlo, sucked up his little pot belly, and, in his deep, somewhat nasal voice, said, "Malcolm, we ain't leavin'. I know how to handle a pistol and a rifle. Spent two years in the Polish army before I came over here. Shot three men once in a border skirmish with the Russians. Give me a gun and I'll fight with you!"

Malcolm, surprised at the revelation by the diminutive Lazlo, was nevertheless grateful for his offer.

"Thanks. Both of you. This isn't your fight, but I certainly can't handle it alone. We need to figure out how we can all get out of here alive!"

Angus woke up with a throbbing headache. It was pitch black. For a few minutes he couldn't remember where he was. He sensed movement and realized that he was in a mine cart lying on top of someone else.

He pulled himself up, rolled out onto the ground and reached back, groping to see if he could determine who his companion was.

"Peg Leg!" he exclaimed when he encountered the tell-tale wooden limb. "It's me, Angus! You're layin' in a mine cart. Are you hurt?"

"Dad gummed right I'm hurt! My head's about to bust! Feels like someone like to knocked my ear off! It's bleedin' all over the place!" Peg Leg moaned as he struggled to get out of the cart. "What happened? Why are we in here in the dark? I smell dynamite. Did the explosion knock us down? I can't figure it out!"

"I was layin' on top of you when I woke up," Angus explained, trying to determine in his own mind just exactly what had happened. "The pistoleros must've slugged you while you was placin' your charges. They threw you in the cart and came for me. I got the same treatment. There's a goose egg as big as your fist on the back of my head. It's a wonder they didn't kill me. I'll bet I laid there a half an hour after I woke up trying to get my bearings. Then you moved--I didn't even know 'till then that you were under me. That's when I finally came around and got out of the cart."

"Where do you figure we're at?" Peg Leg asked as his mind cleared.

"I can feel the end of the track. They shoved us all the way to the end then set off the dynamite. We're sealed in here. It would take a week to dig out if we had picks and shovels, which we don't. There's no food or water. They took my candles and my .44. I'll bet they took yours, too. We won't last four or five days," Angus, resigned to their fate, spoke with the voice of a doomed man.

"We ain't dead yet!" Peg Leg burst out angrily. "I didn't get this old livin' my whole life around claim jumpers and bushwhackers without doin' a few things right. First of all, you're wrong about the water. There's a canteen full of it here. They took my gun but not my water. It holds two quarts. Ought to last us for two or three days since we're not exposed to the sunlight here. Then, I just found two torches in the bottom of the cart. I was layin' right on top of 'em. You're right about one

199

thing. It would take a week or more to dig out with picks and shovels, which we don't have. But, with dynamite, I could blast us out of here."

"Well, that sounds great, but you and I both know we don't have the slightest chance in the world in coming up with any dynamite. Don't tell me they obliged us by leaving some of that in the cart, too?" Angus asked, knowing what the answer would be.

"No, they didn't. But, lookee here. I told you I was a survivor," Peg Leg chortled with glee and lit one of the torches. Angus's eyes widened as Peg Leg unharnassed his hollow wooden leg and dumped its' contents into the cart. He couldn't believe it! Lying before him were three sticks of dynamite with caps and fuses!

Peg Leg continued his suprises by pulling a few slices of jerky out of his money belt. "I always carry a stash of emergency food along," he explained. "Never know when a feller might need it! Now, let's see what we've got to do. We'll have to dig a lot of this rubble out by hand, then try to build up a tunnel if we can find some beams that ain't blown to pieces. That'll give me a crawl space so I can get back in there and figure out where to set these charges. It's dangerous and I might blow us up with the dynamite,but, it's the only chance we got. You'll have to dig in there and find some beams. I can't even lift 'em they're so big."

"Don't worry about it. I can handle it!" a rejuvenated Angus exclaimed and began moving the mountain of rubble with his bare hands. "If you want to save light, just put out that torch. I can feel my way around. We don't need all our air burned up, anyway."

"Good thinkin'," replied Peg Leg as he extinguished the torch. "See if you can dig out a little cavern about fifty yards back there and shore it up with timbers. That'll give me the space I need. While you're doin' that, I'll move the small stuff so we have room to get around."

Up on the bluff, Malcolm, Frank, and Lazlo were loading their weapons.

"There's eight of them and three of us," Frank said. "We don't have a lot of ammunition to spare. Looks like it might be a long day. Realistically, what do you think our chances are?"

" I never dreamed that we'd be facing a gun battle this soon," Malcolm answered and pitched a .30-.06 lever action Springfield to Lazlo. "I've got a hunch that if we take out the claim jumpers, all the fight will go out of the pistoleros. They'd realize there wouldn't be any more paychecks, so they'd probably high tail it. Looks to me like I'd better sneak down there with my .44. It's pretty accurate up to about fifty yards. You boys can cover me with the rifles from that rock pile. As soon as the cave-ins stop and the dust settles, they'll probably come out of that draw and go back to check out the mine. I'll be layin' over by the water trough. That's within my range and they'll be sittin' ducks. I'll tell 'em to lay down their guns. If they open up on me, I'll go for the claim jumpers. You can open up on the pistoleros. If they start runnin', let 'em go. They aren't worth foolin' with. Does that sound OK?"

"You've got it figured out. Lazlo and I will cover you. At that range, we shouldn't have any problems, right Lazlo?" Frank asked.

Lazlo nodded and Malcolm started down the bluff.

In the mine, Angus had made a tremendous discovery!

"Hey!" he yelled to Peg Leg. "Get a torch lit and come in here! Forget about diggin'! As you know, some blasts work in weird ways. There's a long tunnel already exposed once you get through this first layer of debris. Look at this," he directed Peg Leg who was coming in with the torch. "Don't you think I'm right?"

"By George!" Peg Leg exclaimed. "Looks like the blast piled all the big stuff over on the far side and left this whole thing wide open for forty feet or so. If I can direct a charge toward the entrance, I might be able to bust us out with one blast. The problem is, the back blast will kill us unless we build a strong barrier between us and the explosion. I'll start figurin' out just where to place the dynamite and you start buildin' a mountain between it and us. Use the biggest chunks of ore and timbers you can find. Pile 'em deep and wide. We want all the rock we can find piled between us and the blast. If it works, the energy'll be directed towards the entrance. When I'm done, I'll light the fuse and get back over the barricade. If you've piled enough rock, and, if I've guessed right, we just may get out of here shortly. If either of us are wrong, this mine'll collapse and we'll never see daylight again! I want to set off the charge in less than an hour. The mine gas leakin' in here isn't goin' to give us much more time. It's just as deadly as dynamite since we're not gettin' any fresh air to breathe."

Angus, ignoring his still sore ribs, attacked the debris with a vengeance, leaving Peg Leg to marvel at his raw power. The giant Scot tossed boulders big enough to stagger four men as though they were melons.

"Holy mackerel!" Peg Leg cried. "You'll move all the rock before I ever get the dynamite placed! I'd better get to movin'!"

Outside, Malcolm lay by the watering trough. He was only a few yards from the gulch and could hear bits of Sy and Bob's conversation with the Mexicans. They were worried about mine gas and weren't going to enter the mine for another hour. They seemed content to stay where they were, cool in the shade.

Malcolm wasn't as fortunate as he was directly exposed to the desert sun. Forty-five minutes drug by and he felt like he was being baked alive. Something stung his leg. He reached down, grabbed his pant leg, and felt something crawling on his hand. He looked and saw an army of foraging red ants swarming over his boots. Struggling to keep his head down, he kicked and squirmed, trying to thwart their attack. The ants marched on, up his pant legs and into his shirt. Soon his body was covered with a mass of angry welts. Rivulets of sweat cascaded down his body, searing the welts while he writhed in silent agony.

His wait ended moments later when Sy and his men came up out of the gulch.

"Freeze in your tracks and drop those guns!" Malcolm bellowed. "You don't have a chance!"

His command was ignored. The entire group fell on their bellies, pulled their weapons and opened fire!

Malcolm got off one round before ducking. The bullet struck home, exploding Bob's knee cap. His legs gave way, leaving him screaming on the ground as the battle raged on.

Two pistoleros, seeing that Malcolm was pinned down, charged the trough. Frank and Lazlo opened up with a deadly volley. The pistoleros went down without a sound.

"Run for the mine!" Sy shrieked. "There's riflemen on the bluff!"

Malcolm rose to one knee and triggered off several rounds. The first two went wild. The third hit Sy, ripping into his side. He stumbled to his knees and watched helplessly while another of his men fell in the crossfire.

"Help me!" he screamed. Two pistoleros jerked him up and dragged him to the mine.

Inside, Peg Leg detonated his dynamite, sending hundreds of jagged chunks of ore whistling toward the entrance. Sy and his companions, thinking they were running to safety, were mowed down as though hit by grape shot.

Malcolm raced to the scene. Frank and Lazlo showed up moments later. A quick look told them that Bob, who lay fifty yards away wrapping a tourniquet above his wounded knee, was the only survivor.

"What caused that explosion?" Frank asked. "Can't have come from our men. They wouldn't have any dynamite."

"I don't know, but I'm goin' in!" Malcolm exclaimed. "We've got to find out if they're alive!"

"Look no further!" a voice shouted back, followed by the dirt-covered bodies of Peg Leg and Angus who were stumbling through the debris. "What'd you think of that last charge I set off? Wasn't that a humdinger?" Peg Leg asked. "Dad burn near killed Angus and me, but, here we are!"

CHAPTER 29

AN ENDING AND A BEGINNING

It took three months in Washington for Frank to secure the government contracts necessary to guarantee the success of the Rose Pit Mine. Shortly thereafter, the family moved to Alexander.

The townspeople were planning a bittersweet party. Sweet because they would be welcoming a new, handsome family, a great addition to the community. Bitter because the town would be bidding, at least on a short term basis, farewell to Malcolm, Steffi, and their boys. They were moving to Arizona Territory. Malcolm, since he had a major stake in its' success, would be taking over the mining operations. A corporation was formed naming him President. In addition, he'd been appointed Vice-Chairman of the board at the bank, an honorary position he could handle by letters and telegrams.

Jim and Molly leased the Wandering S. It provided them an opportunity to significantly increase their earnings.

"We'll never sell the ranch. We love this place," Malcolm consoled Steffi. "We're not leaving forever. Mines play out sooner or later, but the land is always here. Jim's happy to run it for us until we get back. He's goin' to need some help and I suggested he talk to Raymond. That boy would make a good hand even though he's still pretty young. Jim could teach him a lot. Who knows, might turn him into a foreman someday. As far as coming back for visits--if we have the time--we'll come back for some of the bank's quarterly board meetings. Look at it this way. Leaving Kansas for a while isn't all that bad. Arizona territory is a great, wide-open country and the boys'll learn to love it there. Tombstone's a pretty good town, and it only takes a few days to get up to Tucson. I think you'll really like it out there."

Angus would also be leaving Alexander. He'd let Malcolm talk him into a Vice President/General Manager's job based on the condition that he could spend more time in the mine than in the office. However, like the Frazier's, he was leaving some roots in Kansas. His hired man would keep the blacksmith shop operating while he was gone.

Peg Leg was coming along, too. He was tickled pink with his new job as mine foreman.

"First real job I ever had," he'd said when Malcolm made the offer. "Maybe now I'll settle down now and earn a steady living. I only got about fifteen more good years and I've got to make the most of 'em! Only thing is, miners is a real rowdy bunch. I want Angus to be around anytime I need help to knock some heads. I've got a hunch they'll listen to him!"

Lazlo was moving down from Tombstone and would handle all surveying work plus he offered his accounting skills to help Steffi with her responsibilities as company Treasurer.

"I need all the help I can get!" Steffi said, welcoming Lazlo's offer. "Riding herd on these boys is enough to wear me out."

At the bank, Ben was named Chairman Of The Board, an honorary position. Frank, as president, would actually run the institution.

Ben and Su Chang were working on plans for a new restaurant--sort of a road house/inn between Tombstone and the mine--realizing there would soon be a tremendous build up of business in the area. But, they wondered if their idea would ever get off the ground. Staffing the place was going to be a problem. It would be hard for them to leave Kansas with their current business requiring attention and they would need strong management to open run an Arizona operation. None of their employees wanted to move.

When Malcolm told him he might send Peg Leg down to Nogales to negotiate the release of Lupe and her children from their contract with Don Diego, Ben was elated!

"That's the least we could do for Smooth Mouth and the boys," he exclaimed. "That's what they wanted. If Peg Leg can secure their freedom, I could provide jobs for all of them."

Peg Leg went to Nogales. Don Diego gladly released the family in exchange for the stack of U.S. currency that Peg Leg laid out, money provided by Malcolm and Ben. When they arrived in Alexander, Ben put the family up at the Inn. Soon Lupe was cooking on the day shift and the girls were waiting tables. Pedro found a friend in Raymond and began helping him with his duties around the inn.

After a week, pleased to see that Lupe had a natural talent for leadership as well as being an excellent cook, Ben discussed his plans with her. She readily agreed to take her family to Arizona if he built a new restaurant, delighted that it would only be about seventy miles to Nogales.

A street dance was planned for Saturday night, the weekend that Frank and his family would arrive in Alexander. The timing couldn't have been better since the Frazier's and Angus would be departing the following week. The town had found a perfect reason to blow off steam with an old fashioned, double-barreled jubilee!

On Saturday afternoon, a first class rodeo featuring cowboys from as far south as Texas was staged at a makeshift grandstand behind the stockyards.

Malcolm loved to ride saddle broncs but decided not to participate. He didn't want to be nursing any broken bones on the trip west. He and Steffi, wanting to get to know them better, sat with Frank and Penelope. Little Colin and Hugh were playing in a sandpile under the stands, entertaining the two year old Peck twins, Karen and Karla, beautiful little blonds with curls tumbling to their shoulders who were thrilled with the attention they were getting.

Malcolm smiled when he noticed Raymond sporting a new felt cattleman's hat. The youth was swaggering just a bit as he mixed with the crowd, letting the word out that he'd soon be working on the Frazier ranch.

Dirty Bart and Little Bert were entered in the bronc-riding contest and, much to everyone's delight, won their events over the Texas cowboys. They stopped to say goodbye to Malcolm and Steffi, making it known that they and their guns would be available if Malcolm ever had any trouble at the mine.

J. T. Smith stopped by to shake their hands and said, "Guess I should have tried to hang onto that mining stock a little longer. Looks like you boys are flat out going to get rich! Well, it's like I told the missus, if there's any easy deals out there they usually pass me by! But, I've got no hard feelings. Might even want to start a mercantile store down in that country one of these days. Looks like a lot of business could be had!"

That night, as they slow danced under the stars, Malcolm and Steffi were engulfed in their own emotions as memories of the Wandering S and their days in Alexander flooded over them. Neither said a word for a long time, then, seeing a shooting star across the cloudless sky, Malcolm paused, pointed to it while he embraced a now sobbing Steffi, kissed her for a long time, then, slowly, ever so slowly, began moving again to the music.

ABOUT THE AUTHOR

Ernie Frazier, a grandson of Kansas pioneers who came west in a covered wagon, was raised near old Dodge City, the infamous cowtown that helped make the west wild.

He has also lived in Arizona and Texas and travels extensively in many of the areas he writes about, touring mines and ancient ruins in the U. S. and Mexico.

His experiences-some of which are vividly revisited in his writings-provide much of his inspiration. As a young soldier he was exposed to the underbelly of life while stationed on the Arizona-Mexican border. Later he began a career which provides financial products and services to estate and business owners. His knowledge of banking comes from having served on a bank's board of directors, feeding cattle, and by selling operating businesses to investors.

CPSIA information can be obtained
at www.ICGtesting.com
Printed in the USA
FFOW03n0846010316
21979FF